THE MISSOURI DOGMAN AND OTHER TALES OF MIDWEST MACABRE

BRETT THARP

CONTENTS

The Missouri Dogman   1

Among The Levees   23

River Song   37

The People In The Fort   51

The Needle   63

Midwest Macabre   71

UNDER A FUNERAL MOON   79
With Micah S. Vernon

THROUGH THE BLACK SALOON

Prologue   113

Chapter One   121

Chapter Two   131

Acknowledgments   135

About the Author   137

THE MISSOURI DOGMAN

He came to them no better than a stray mutt, shambling up the wild dirt roads of southern Missouri in a late August heat. He came beaten, he came thirsty, he came without fortune with the west at his back. He came alone.

Old Bob Peeker watched the man make his approach up what passed for main street in the town of Wilder. He perched forward atop his bucket seat, watching, wishing for a rocking chair but Colson Knapp was charging too much to build him one. Four times as much as he would ever pay, in fact. He took the newcomer for a vagrant at a hundred yards and nothing he learned at any ensuing distance judged Old Bob wrong in that regard.

The vagrant caught sight of him and made his way over. His steps were short, feet strangely close together. "What they sellin' in there I can buy with four pennies?" the vagrant asked.

"Cain't even get you a coca-cola. Cost a nickel," Old Bob said.

The vagrant nodded, thinking.

"What you doin' here? Passin' on? Headed to California?"

The vagrant shook his head, his wild black hair sending out a cloud of dust. All of him was filthy, like he'd been sleeping in dirt. "Naw, I been to California already. Gettin' crowded out there. Could use a bit of work though. Know of any?"

The general store owner, Tom Stone, stepped out then and looked the vagrant up and down with an unfriendly eye. "What's this?"

"You sell a coca-cola for four pennies or a nickel?" the vagrant said.

"A nickel. What you doin' here, boy?"

"Feller lookin' for work he said," Old Bob said. "I was fixin' to say Mr. Milton's only one probably hirin'."

"Maybe," Tom said, not taking his eyes off the vagrant.

"Hey, you got some dog food in there I can buy?"

"Sure, but it's a nickel."

"Hell. What about cat food?"

"I can sell you that for three pennies. You got a dog?"

"Naw."

Tom looked at him for a long time, and Old Bob did too. Finally Tom went inside and came back out with the can of cat food and passed it to the vagrant. Tom looked at the pennies in the palm of his hand and flipped them. Old Bob peeked in and saw that the coins were so coated with dried mud you could barely tell what kind they were.

"Where's Mr. Milton at?"

"Farm's a few miles down the road, way you was already headed. Big house is kinda far back in the boonies. Snake fuckin' road, twisted practically round on itself."

"You got an extra penny I'll give ya a look at a map," Tom put in.

"I'll find it, thank ya." The vagrant packed the cat food

away in his pocket and continued up main street. The two men watched until he was out of sight.

"You get that feller's name?" Tom asked.

"No, I didn't wanna know it." They existed there in a warm silence for a time, then Tom went back inside, the threshold laid bare after him to let the air in. Old Bob said, "I shoulda knowed there was somethin' wrong with that feller minute I saw him. There's just somethin' about a man walkin' east alone in nineteen thirty an' nine." He shook his head to himself, unbothered that no one was listening, and put it from mind, as a man did with all the things he could not change.

———

THE DOGS WARNED of his approach long before he appeared from the deep brush at the forest line. Jerry Bell jumped when they set to baying madly from their pen, jumped so bad the guitar he'd been picking almost went careening out of hand across the grass. He looked up and caught sight of the boy as he came tramping out of the wood, squinting into the barbed sunlight and coming on heedlessly. "Hey, Lou," he called."Get a load of this shit."

Louis Lee, who was second only to Mr. Milton, came over to Jerry and watched the boy approach the barbed wire fence. What they saw was the first of many queer things they would see the boy do. Rather than climb over the wires, or spread them with boot and hand in the middle to climb through, he got down on his belly in a bald spot where it had been dug out by the comings and goings of hounds and slithered under. "I'll be damned," Louis said.

"Where you think he learned that?" Jerry asked.

"From a dog, I imagine. Ole boy musta growed up with mutts. Gotta be."

The dogs still screamed alarm, but the men saw nothing fearsome in the vagrant boy as he crossed by the barn. The place was emptied of all but them, as it was Sunday, and Mr. Milton liked to take the kids to church. He came up to them, slit-eyed, and said, "I heard you all might have some work for me."

"We won't be talkin' work til I know your name, feller," Louis said, studying him. The boy smelled, but it wasn't so much a bad smell as it was a *wild* smell. He smelled like he'd come from the woods, as they knew he had, but Louis Lee couldn't figure that there was anything wrong with that, though it did niggle at him some. Later, he would think that it wasn't that he smelled of the woods, it was that he smelled like he'd been in the woods his whole life and never bathed it off him except in a creek or pond.

"Call me Bob Crawford." The boy put out his hand and Louis took it and felt the calluses and the dust on it.

"Louis Lee. That there is Jerry Bell."

"I figured you was Mr. Milton. He abouts? Need me a job."

"He's at church. You can talk to me. I'm close to a boss as a man can be here who ain't named Milton, but he'll be the last word on it."

"Well I'm happy to talk to ya then."

"What can ya do?"

"I done just about everything I reckon."

"Well this is a farm so how about the stuff farmers do?"

"Planted corn, tossed hay, picked cotton and tomata's and watermelons and squash, minded all sort o' animals, cows and pigs and chickens and goats. Took care of a horse for a few days. Even got in the seat of a tractor once."

"Well we ain't got no tractors so don't you worry about that."

Jerry Bell piped up. "Here comes boss man."

A dust cloud sprouted up in the distance above the road, thrice the height of the car that birthed it. Though it hadn't rained in weeks, all of them had sweat running down their faces and under their loose shirts and it was a rotten insult that it could be so humid without rain. The car, black and glossy when it was purchased but now painted brown with dust and dried mud, turned onto and climbed the subtle slope of the driveway and parked beside them up against the big house. The boy flew out of the car first and went tumbling through the grass, squealing in his Sunday best. The girl followed, reserved and prim, and Crawford looked at her steadily for two instants too long before he turned to study the tall man getting out on the driver side. The girl slowed as she passed, looking at the stranger curiously, but Louis gave her a look and she hurried into the house.

Francis Milton looked younger than his forty years, and he dressed well for church if for little else. His coal black hair was shiny and splashed across his scalp and he kept his jaw freshly shaven every single morning. A noble soul, he gave every man a chance.

Crawford stuck out his hand to Milton and Milton shook it, proffering his question only with a direct look and the tilt of his eyebrows. "Names Bob Crawford, sir. I reckon you're Mr. Milton? I'm after a job."

"What can you do, sir?"

Crawford gave the same explanation he had just given to Louis and Jerry. At the end of it, Milton nodded and said, "Hired. Jerry, why don't you show him around and see him to the bunkhouse."

They went together, and when they were out of earshot, Louis said to Milton, "You sure about that? There's something off about that feller. Shoot, you shoulda seen the way he-"

"Lou, we just don't have the circumstances to be turning away a hand right now. We need every body we can get. If he doesn't work out, then he doesn't work out. I can tolerate oddity if it gets the work done." Milton studied Crawford's back at a distance. "How strange can a man seeking gainful employment in these dark days be? And can someone shut those damn dogs up already?"

———

JERRY BELL PLUCKED at the old guitar gently, meandering his way toward the end of a song he was never going to finish. The bunkhouse was half-empty, two other hands playing cards at the table in dim light, a third fast asleep already with an open magazine laid across his chest. The door sprawled open and pale light that shimmered from the passing of wispy clouds over the moon laid its threshold long and dancing across the floor.

Louis Lee appeared there suddenly to scan the room for a second before crossing over to his bed, perpendicular to Jerry's. "Why don't you play something someone'll wanna hear, Jerry?"

"Never was one for learnin' other folk's songs," he said.

"Rate you're going you'd better start takin' that guitar and play for the chickens. We ain't ever gonna hear the end of it elsewise."

"Yeah, maybe."

Louis scanned the room again. "Where's Crawford?"

"Ain't seen him. You're around him a whole lot more'n me. How's he been doin'?"

"Alright. Don't listen too good, sometimes, but when he gets to it he does his part. He's got somethin' with cows though, they mind him like no other I ever seen."

A shadow came down across the floor. They looked up and saw in the doorway a shape black and faceless with the pale, shimmering light gone still along the lines of its silhouette with the growing, glowing moon beyond it. It stepped into the light and they saw none other than Bob Crawford, and who else might it have been in any case? Only a man, only the one missing.

They had managed to bathe him and his clothes were clean, but he still had a wild smell to him. A wild look too, undomesticated even, like someone had turned out a bobcat among a pack of housecats. He went to his bunk, two down from Jerry, and sat and studied the men playing cards. They didn't acknowledge him. They knew better than to establish anything with a new hand when he could be gone the next day. "Where ya been, Crawford?" Louis asked him.

Bob swung to look at him. "Just out at the barn. Them kids was playing out there."

"Both of 'em?" His voice was granite and his eyes cold as he looked at him.

"Yessir. Hey, I seen that boy going out to the woods at the south end. Seemed kinda far for a young'n to be."

"He ain't s'posed to be out there. Been warned lord knows how many times."

"I'll tell 'im if I see 'im there again."

"Both kids was out there?"

"Huh?"

"Both kids was out at the barn playin' just now? The girl and the boy?"

"Well I'm pretty sure the boy was in the loft some-wheres, I heard him playin'. The girl come out a little after, said she was having a tea party."

Louis regarded him stonily. The men at the table had pricked their ears up, but did not look. He spoke slowly. "She said, huh. How old's that girl?"

"What?"

"How old is that girl? Tell me. Best guess."

Crawford thought on it. "Well . . . looked thirteen or so."

Louis fixed his gaze hard on Crawford and they stared at each other for several long moments. To his credit, Crawford didn't look away. "You got that right," Louis said. He lay back in bed and stared at the ceiling. The bunk had a short, uncomfortable silence as the vagrant's eyes hung on Louis for a moment, but it broke just as quickly as Crawford turned and went off the bed.

"Heard you was in California before?" Jerry said.

He shrugged. "For a time."

"How was it? Must be a lot of folks out there now."

"I'm sure it treated a lot of 'em better'n it did me."

Later, in the darkest hours of night, Jerry came to in a feeble daze. Reluctant to open his eyes and make final his awakening, he listened to the quiet snores and the sounds outside for a time. Gentle as a kiss, he heard footsteps behind him, moving away. He turned his head and looked weakly at the doorway, still open wide, that soon filled with the outline of a man going out into the night. Again, the shimmering light stilled around it and the wild seemed to hush.

―――――

THE TAWNY HOUND shied from his hand and whimpered, but he saw the flecks of blood on its neck. It backed away toward the other end of the pen and lay down, head flat against the earth, looking at him big and scared. Louis squatted there forward on his toes, softly nudging the other excited dogs away, watching the biggest of them cowed. The others swarmed anxiously around, as if lost.

"Had to'a happened this morning with blood still in his fur," he said.

Jerry leaned over the fence behind him. "Yeah. Crazy thing, I cain't tell which one of 'em done it. Not a one o' the others showin' blood. None of 'em acting like they's boss neither."

They were silent for a long time. The dogs calmed and lay down or trotted about aimlessly. "You read the paper?" Jerry asked.

"Naw." Louis Lee hated every word the paper men wrote. He thought it was nothing but government talk and government talk was dirt to him.

"Said them Germans invaded Poland. They's war in Europe."

"Don't give a shit. Ain't no war here."

"Don't know where Poland is exactly . . . but it cain't be good. Maybe we'll go to war too. My boy always wanted to be a soldier, but weren't no war to fight. He'd sign up in a second." Jerry remembered the other news he had that had been dulled by the new war. "Ole Bob said Tom Stone's got broke into. Pack o' wild dogs got into his stock, ate up his dog an' cat food."

"I heard some talk 'bout them dogs. They're gettin' into everybody's shit."

"Yep."

"A feller broke in?"

"Had to'a, but only stuff taken were stuff that was ate. Didn't take no money."

"Hell."

Crawford marched by, carrying a bale of hay. He grinned crazily at them. The dogs regarded him warily and not one of them barked as he passed.

———

Francis Milton was a godly man and he believed no Christian soul should work on a Sunday. So on Saturday night, the men drank and carroused and had an all around good time that they could sleep off the next day before work resumed on Mondays. From beneath the floorboards of the bunkhouse they produced crates of cheap beer and jars of moonshine and drank away the weariness of the week. Jerry Bell plugged away at his guitar to an audience of none and an audience of all, and the rest stood around the fire chattering. Most of the talk was of Europe and the night bore a strange cold too fierce for the season.

Louis Lee silently counted heads and noticed that Bob Crawford was absent. He went into the bunkhouse and seeing Crawford was missing there too, he went out to check the barn. There remained a mutual distance between Crawford and the other men, neither side wanting to break the peace and make friends. To Louis that was confirmation that Crawford had no intention of lingering long with them, and his already low charitability to the strange young man would run shorter in future, accordingly.

The barn was pitch black, but Crawford detached from the shadows on his approach and watched him, pelvis thrust out and thumbs hanging over the rims of his pockets. Louis stopped and studied him for a moment before speaking. The vagrant's whole attitude seemed to shift at night, like he was more comfortable with it than the daylight. Just another thing Louis decided he didn't like about him. "Whatchu doin' in there, boy?"

"Gave the milk cow some more feed. She seemed hungry. Sweet animal." Crawford's eyes were shaded ominously by his hat, the moon at his back, but Louis knew he wore his usual expression, the one that outwardly offered nothing but somehow rang of contempt to him. He sensed that the boy thought nothing of him, nothing at all, and it galled him.

"She gets enough. Don't you worry about her now, get on." Louis started to turn away.

"She was hungry. You orta get off my back some. I've given you no cause to be, I work hard as any man."

He turned back, tried to find something in the shadows over the young man's face. He thought he saw a spark where the eyes should be, something that glinted briefly like gold. "I'm gonna tell you something now, Crawford, I don't care for ya. You got a insolence an' I know you won't last here."

"That ain't up to you though is it? You not no boss. You just the boss's boy, same as the rest of us."

Louis' cheeks flushed with heat and his hand curled into a fist at his side. He liked the idea of putting the boy on his ass, but he stifled it. He had to be bigger than that. He stepped closer and his voice came out low and danger-ous. "I see you, boy. You just another drifter come crawling back from California, broke. You'll be gone in a week, two maybe. Get as far as you can on the dollars we give ya. They won't last neither. And next year I'll forget you were ever a person." They stared at each other for several long moments. When it was clear Crawford wouldn't respond, he said, "Now get on back. Ain't nothin' for you here in the dark. There's beer an' shine there yonder."

Crawford walked back and Louis followed him the whole way. "Zed," he called to the thin man by the beer crate. "Get this feller somethin' to drink." Zed reached in and produced a beer and tossed it to Crawford. Crawford looked down at it for a moment, then took it over to Jerry where he sat playing.

He went down on his knees like a child and listened to the aimless plucking for a time. "Why don'tcha play somepin happy? Like to make a feller sad listenin' to you."

Jerry chuckled. "On'y songs I know are mine and mine're sad cuz I'm sad I guess."

"Whatchu got to be sad about? Got a job, got your guitar. Pretty slick gig what I seen."

"Miss my boy, miss my woman. That's the jist of it I s'pose."

"Where they at?"

"My woman died 'bout six years back. Took ill and never got better. My boy went out west after that, but I couldn't stand to leave her where I cain't visit her every day." He paused. "Used to be I could play any song under the sun. Heard a thing once and I could play it. My woman, she said I orta try writing somethin' and so I been tryin' but it ain't come through all the way yet."

Crawford just looked up at him and said, "Well don't you stop tryin'."

They continued like that for half an hour, then Teddy Sanders called over to Crawford, "Hey Bob, come on over here, fella."

Crawford got that wild, hunted look in his eyes, but he came and stood by them around the fire. He was still nursing his beer where the others had all downed several each. That was all it took to break down the wall between them.

"You was out in California right?"

"Yessir."

"How was it?" The others, Zed and Louis and Joe Sawyer, listened intently. They were all loosened and inquisitive under the touch of drink, all but Joe, who instead tended to grow morose.

"Whatchu wanna know?"

"Well how was the jobs an' the land? Folks said they was hunnerds and thousands o' jobs working the prettiest land you ever would see. I didn't believe none of it but most o' them folks didn't come back. Guess they still out there workin'."

"You really wanna know the truth?"

Teddy shuffled his feet. "Why sure."

"Weren't nothin' like they said it was, that I'll tell ya. They was work but ya had to fight a thousand folks for every job and never could hold down one for long 'cause the bosses'd sell your spot to someone for cheaper. Work one job for twenty cents an hour, then someone else take it for fifteen next week. Pay a thousand men pick a field clean in a few days for next to nothin' and cut 'em loose. The land was pretty enough, that's true." He looked into the flames as he spoke and they sparked back in his eyes, dancing on the irises. "Saw folks killed and burnt out. Cops'd come and break up their camps with guns and look for a fight. If they got one then men'd come back after dark and set fire to everything they could an' the next day folks'd just build back. Nothin' else to do. Folks'd protest the wages and get beat damn near to death in a ditch."

They were silent for a time. Teddy chuckled nervously to break the quiet. "Aw you're foolin'. Cain't be like that. Hardly none o' them folks came back."

"What they s'posed to come back to? Probably couldn't afford the gas to come back anyhow. A hunnerd thousand folks out there stranded 'thout work nor gas nor food. Half of 'em probably starved to death by now. California's a graveyard now I figure."

Big Joe Sawyer spoke up. "You're lyin'. My brother went out there, I know'd he'd find work. You're lyin'."

"You ain't been out there, how'd you know?" Crawford demanded. There was something in his tone, underneath the irritation. Bitterness.

"He sends me letters ever' month, swears he's doin' fine. Says he got more work than he knows what to do with. Says loads of folks doin' fine."

"Might be so for him, but that ain't what I saw. An' I was out there two years. Maybe he's lyin' so you won't worry for him."

"Yeah. Well I say you're the damn liar, boy." Big Joe stood up and spat on the floor in Crawford's direction. The vagrant hesitated, then delivered another one of his crazy grins.

"Well I say you're an idiot."

Teddy tried to halt Joe's sudden approach, but Joe was twice his size and he thrust Teddy aside easily. Crawford tried to dodge back, but Joe's hand shot out swift as a snake and snatched the front of his shirt and pulled him back in. He reared back with one fist and slammed it straight into Crawford's nose. The boy slumped under the blow, his head rocking back sickeningly. Joe jerked him back up and hit him twice more. Crawford's mouth and chin were bathed red by the stream from his nose. He hung there, dazed and half-limp, in Joe's grip for a few moments as Joe halted his assault. The big man looked around, grinning madly at the horror on their faces. "He ast for it. You heard him call my brother a liar. I owed it to 'im."

He felt hands take hold of his shirt at both shoulders. When he turned back to look at Crawford, all he saw was the boy's open jaws darting at his face.

Crawford bit deep into Joe's nose and dug in and ripped away viciously, tearing away the majority of it and a great deal of flesh around it besides. Joe let go of Crawford's shirt and lurched back, shrieking. Crawford threw back his head wildly, sending out an arc of blood to fleck the men's faces, then spat the wad of flesh and cartilage into the flame. He bared his crimson-washed teeth and in the surging violence of the moment it cast a ghastly, bestial visage at the stunned onlookers.

Joe went down on his knees and cradled the gory ruin of his face in his hands, choking out strangled sobs. Teddy and Zed stepped away from him, unsure what to do. Crawford only stood there, teeth bared, watching the maimed man crying. His face twisted from that crazy grin into something that resembled a snarl.

Jerry Bell slammed him over the head from behind with his guitar. The instrument shattered inward around Crawford's skull and snapped where the neck joined the body, but the boy went down and did not rise again. The strings twanged discordantly in the moment of the strike.

"Shit, shit, shit," Jerry said. "I didn't kill 'im, did I?"

"He'll live," Louis said, suddenly overtaken with weariness from his eyes down to his feet. "Zed, help me get him out to the barn. We'll lock him in there 'til Mr. Milton decides what's to be done. Better find some rope or twine or somethin'. Teddy, do somethin' about Joe." They took up Crawford at each end and toted him awkwardly out towards the barn. Joe still sobbed, and Teddy went down beside him and murmured something.

Jerry only stood there and watched. To himself, he said, "What a fuckin' mess."

———

"SIT DOWN, Louis, for God's sake," Mr. Milton said, exasperated.

Louis Lee had hung near the door even after being invited in, his hat held over his stomach, as he told the tale. Mr. Milton had taken a seat at the dinner table and listened. When it was done he stared at the wood of the table and ran his hand through his hair and was silent for a time before the outburst. Louis sat awkwardly across from him, perching his hat on his knee beneath the table. He couldn't stop doing things with his hands, picking at nails and tapping on the meat of his thighs, so he threaded his fingers tightly together in his lap.

"I guess I should've listened to you," Mr. Milton said with a mirthless chuckle. "You said the boy was strange on day one."

"I didn't see this comin'. Nobody could," Louis said, wanting to take the burden back.

"Where'd you put him?"

"Out in the barn, locked tight. He's out cold, will be for a while, but we tied 'im anyway. Jerry hit him a good one."

"And Joe?"

"Lord, I . . . I don't know what you do after that. That boy bit his whole damn nose off. Ain't nothin' normal after that."

Mr. Milton nodded. "I don't know what to do about this boy. I really don't."

"I know what your ole Pa would do."

"He'd bury that boy by the river tonight. Those were the old times. These days it's best to leave it up to the law."

"What the hell would they do? Throw him in jail for a

bit, turn him loose later. This boy is an animal, he ain't like us. Who else'd he do this to? Who else *has* he done it to?"

Mr. Milton didn't answer immediately. They sat in silence for what felt close to ten minutes before he finally said, "I need the word of God in my heart before I make such a decision. I'm taking my children to church in the morning. When I return . . . we will do something."

In the deep darkness of the barn, shut away from the world, the cow lifted its head when it heard a desperate scratching in the far recesses of the building. Something in the shadows snuffled and grunted and growled. The cow shifted nervously and moved to stand as far away as the narrow stall would let her.

———

In the late afternoon, after Mr. Milton and the children returned from church, he had finally come to a decision. Louis and Zed threw the barn doors wide. Louis carried a sixgun at his side and Zed a shotgun. They needn't have bothered, for Bob Crawford was nowhere to be found. In a rear corner of the building, where the dirt was fine and soft like sand, they saw where he had burrowed under the rear wall and scraped through. The rope that had bound him lay in pieces where he had chewed through it.

Francis Milton went pale when they told him. His boy, young Thomas, had been let out to play, Francis secretly hoping he would venture far to not witness nor interfere with what he intended to do. They all knew the boy liked to play in the woods near the barn. Perhaps all of Crawford's vengeance would be directed at Louis or Jerry, but who could say with a boy so unnatural as that? A desperate vagrant willing to bite and eat the flesh of another man might not think twice about killing the boy just for spite, especially if he knew what the father intended?

All the men, armed with their own guns or borrowed from Mr. Milton, assembled outside the bunkhouse. Unwilling even to think that their pursuit might extend past dusk, none dared suggest bringing lanterns. Even Big Joe Sawyer, who had been bedridden through the night and day, staggered from the bunkhouse when he heard. The bandages where his nose had been were soaked through with red and leaking, and he walked unsteadily, but he had his own pistol and pushed Teddy away when he protested.

Jerry turned out the dogs, but when shown the tracks and the ropes that wore Crawford's scent they whimpered and slunk back and would not be pressed forward more than a few yards toward the forest. The men followed the tracks as best they could until they lost them among the thicker brush. The men then spread out at wide intervals at which they could still keep sight of one another and went after him.

The evening whisked by in their pursuit, but dusk was on them long before they turned up any trace of the boy. Jerry shivered against the unseasonal cool and walked on, having to look to his feet to keep from tripping more than seeking a hint of Crawford. The moon beamed huge and powerful through the canopy in places and he was thankful for it. He was now in the wild undergrowth near the river and one overeager step could see a man desperately tangled in the brush in half a heartbeat. The pistol hung loose in his sweaty grip. His teeth chattered, half to the cold and half to the fear that crept up in him. He talked to himself excitedly, "Might have to shoot a feller. Lord, I might have to shoot 'im." He didn't think he could do it. Maybe he would forget to cock the hammer back, or maybe his finger would simply not be able to pull the trigger if the time came.

He heard something, close, and froze, listening hard. Low growls and snaps and yips came through a high spread of brush, and he knew he was near the river by the sound of running water. He crept closer and moved to push the branches aside. A hand clamped around his mouth and pulled him back. He grunted and grabbed at the hand but stopped when Louis' voice whispered, "Shh, it's just me. Is it him?" Gently, his grip loosened and disappeared. Jerry looked at him, both of them crouched there like thieves, and nodded. They crept forward together and pried a peephole through the brush.

There lay a clearing at the riverside where they looked, and in it huddled a mass of shuddering forms around the sprawled body of a man. They were dogs, they quickly realized, jittering, excited beasts tearing into the body like wolves born again. They could not tell who the man on the ground was, but there was no sense to hoping he still lived with the way they ravaged him without resistance. Jerry felt his last meal coming up from his gut. Then one of the dogs sat up straight, like a man.

They knew he was chewing, both by the sound of him turning the meat around and around eagerly in his mouth and the silhouette of his jaw working, but the outline of his face was wrong, it was too long. Ears extended over his skull strangely, far too large and pointed at the tip. The creature bent down again to bite. Little about what they saw made sense, but they both knew who it must be. There was only one solution for a beast like this.

"Get that pistol up," Louis whispered. When Jerry was slow to respond, he lifted and half-aimed the gun for him. "When I shoot, you shoot. Dogs'll run soon as they hear a shot. We'll get this sumbitch, Jerry, we'll do it." He hefted his hunting rifle and shifted over a few yards where he had a better view and took aim. Jerry aimed through the bush, shaking so hard he thought he was about to lose the pistol. He couldn't pick a target with that impediment and aimed loosely at the packed mass of shapes. Crawford didn't sit up, didn't give Louis a good shot. Jerry didn't know if Louis would patiently wait for his moment.

He didn't.

The rifle bucked and blasted out a round. One of the dogs yelped and lurched away, tumbling through the grass. The heads of the other beasts and the thing that must be Crawford all shot up in unison, searching for the source. Though they were blackened by the moonlight on their backs, their eyes gleamed bright and yellow and hungry.

The rifle banged again.

Crawford jerked from the hit and the dogs scattered, barking. Jerry's mind shrieked triumph and his teeth ground together in a feral grin, but Crawford didn't fall.

He rose.

He loped across the clearing, and Jerry heard chaos in the brush where Louis was. He couldn't see anything, the branches sweeping back and forth and the air full with growls and screams and sickening tearing. He winced at every agonized shriek, every strangled, inhuman noise that came from their mortal struggle. He moved a few steps closer, terror shooting through his body like lightning. He helplessly thrust the pistol out before him in the direction of the sounds, but there was nothing to shoot, nothing to see. The brush eventually stilled, and the sounds with it.

Crawford emerged into the clearing, walking upright like a man, but Jerry saw how much larger he was than the boy he had briefly known. The skin illuminated on his arm was furred. Jerry found a shot of courage and came out of the forest, pistol upraised. "I'll shoot you, you sumbitch. I'll do it," he growled, hoping it sounded fearsome.

Crawford looked at him over his shoulder and his maw was long like a dog's and the jaws that hung half-open were rowed with teeth pointed like daggers. His ears perked up straight. He coughed strangely. Later, Jerry would realize it was a laugh. Jerry didn't shoot. His finger lay on the trigger, but he didn't do it. He couldn't decide, couldn't find whether he was capable of killing a thing. Crawford crouched low, watching him, then went to all fours and bounded away into the darkness.

The others found Jerry over Louis' body after he dragged it out into the clearing beside the other corpse. He was hoarse from screaming for them. Louis was brutally mauled, but somehow the damage to his body seemed minor next to who they discovered to be Joe Sawyer. He now was missing a throat to match his absent nose, as well as most of his innards having been dug out and devoured.

They never found young Thomas Milton, not his body nor his bones. But on the bank of the river, there by the clearing, they saw footprints. Prints sized to a boy, and around it the innumerable signs of a pack of dogs.

AMONG THE LEVEES

The phone rang, harsh against the silent droning of the night-choked house like a scream. He ignored the first two, finally rolling over towards the nightstand on the third to stare bleary-eyed at the machine. He picked up on the fourth. "Hello?"

"It's John Hadley again, Dan," a woman's voice said.

That's not what John Hadley sounds like. He's a man with a man's voice. He had looked but hadn't really registered the number before picking it up. As he fought through sleep, the name of the voice's owner came to him. "That you, Norma? It's the middle of the night."

"Who on God's green earth did you think it was, Dan? You got caller ID like everyone else."

"What is it?"

"I told you, it's that no good sonofabitch John Hadley. I seen him in my yard again because he had Wesley barking, but when I turned on the porch light he started walking off into the field there on the south end and that damn dog got off after him."

"So what's the problem? Sound like you got a good dog to run off a trespasser that easy."

"He's not GONE! I can hear that boy out there in the levees hollering and I heard Wesley barking out there but now he's stopped and ain't come home."

"What's he hollering?"

"What?"

"What's he yelling about? Was it anything?"

"Same shit he's always going on about, devils in the sky, in the woods, under his bed. I don't know. It turned into nonsense about as quick as it begun."

"Mm."

"I've been calling for him. Wesley I mean. He won't come. I'm damn scared, Dan. You need to come over here and have a look."

He buried the phone in a pillow across the bed and groaned loudly into the silence. He pressed it back to his ear, staring up at the spinning ceiling fan. "It really doesn't sound like he's gonna hurt you, Norma. Just let him be and see if he comes back in the morning. Probably will in time for breakfast. I'll go over to John's and talk to him first thing before I go to work. He just needs to get off the drink is all."

You can't get a parent off a dead child though.

Hadley's boy had turned up floating in one of the drainage ditches out among the backroads the prior year. The idea that went around was that he'd slipped, fell in, and hit his head. He must have, to have drowned in such shallow waters, but it was hard for Dan to reconcile that chain of events, let alone John. There was also the notion of an eight-year-old, far from town and a mile or more from any neighbor, sneaking out so far in total darkness that rubbed like sandpaper.

John had quit his job at the garage within the month

and now only turned up in the public consciousness when he disrupted a neighbor's sleep on one of his benders.

There was a small silence on the other line after he spoke, but it was full of something. Disappointment, certainly, but something else that he somehow felt without it being spoken. "Dan, you promised me if he did this again you'd handle it no matter what time of day or night it was. You promised me that. You know we're far off alone out here, ain't no police to call that'll help a soul in any time at all. Even if there were, I wouldn't trust 'em to."

She was right. He had promised, though he hadn't expected it to come to anything.

She continued. "It's hard being alone out here, Dan. I can't hardly stand it with this kind of a person haunting me."

"I know the feeling, Norma." The bed felt colder around him, and shorter and skinnier and he sank deeper in it, though it was big enough for two. Big for two and far too empty for one.

"No, you don't. It's harder on us old folks. An old woman especially. Only been a year since Jackson . . ." She trailed off.

Cancer is a killer. Though he'd never known it to take a person as fast as it had Jackson. No more than a couple of months, against the doctor's time frame. It seemed like people were dying all too often around here anymore. "What time is it?"

"It's a quarter after one."

"Well expect me there at half past."

"Dan . . . thank you."

"Mmhmm." He hung up.

He hauled himself up to a sitting position and hunched over his knees slightly, breathing slow. His knees popped as he rose, and he stretched long in the shadows of the lonely house before flicking the switch for the lamp on the night-stand. He wrestled into his jeans and made for the laundry room, a pair of rolled white socks dangling from his fist.

He donned a tan coat. It was getting into harvest time, but the nights were unseasonably cold lately. He skipped over his everyday boots and grabbed the rubber pair that rolled up past the knee to go wading. Next to them were a pair of small pink sneakers, almost the right size for a child but not quite. He stared at them for a while, jaw tight, before forcing himself out the door.

The night air kissed him coolly on the porch. He walked out to his pickup and climbed in, slotting in the key and listening to it roar to life. A rock tune burst out of the crackling speakers, and he twisted the volume knob back his way. He'd left the glove box open again, and his check-book lay sprawled across the truck's manual along with a mechanic bill. Tucking them back in the glove box, he checked the gas dial. Under a quarter, but Norma's wasn't far. He backed out onto the gravel road that snaked between his house and Norma's, narrowly missing the mailbox, and headed east toward her place.

The porch lights came on as he pulled in. He turned off the truck and got out, tucking the keys into the pocket of his coat. Norma had manifested behind the screen door, and he took the brick laid walk to the porch steps. He stopped on the top step and waited for her to come all the way out, a small unspoken tradition between them he couldn't remember starting. She thrust the screen door out and took one single step out of the house and held there, the door hanging propped against her robed shoulder. She had always been a pale blonde, but the color was teetering on that line that pushed up against white.

They nursed a long silence together. Finally, she said,

"Might be I ort to have shot him. When I had him in my sights. And not wasted your time."

"Well, who's gonna bury him if you go and do that huh?"

She smiled. "True enough." She motioned and stepped back into the dim house. The lights in the kitchen were on over her shoulder, the other rooms dark. "Come in."

He paused before following through the screen door. He stopped two steps into the house and waited while she went through the dark room to his left into another. When she came back, she had a pistol in her hand. She handed it to him.

He looked down at the snub-nosed revolver. It was tiny in his big hands. "What do I need this for?"

"Well, I'll leave that to you I reckon."

"You think I'm gonna shoot that fool?"

"I wouldn't rat you out if you did, but you can shoot it in the air and scare his ass off if you prefer."

He tried to hand it back. "No thanks."

"Damn it, Dan, take it. That boy is madder than hell. Something's different tonight, I'll be more comfortable if you take it."

"What if he gets around me, comes back here while I'm gone?"

She stared at him. "Well hell, I got more, Dan."

He looked at the gun again. "Well alright." He cracked open the cylinder, saw all six chambers were loaded, then pushed it back into place.

"You got a flashlight?" she asked.

"Yeah, it's in the truck."

"Batteries good?"

"Should be, but I got spares if they ain't."

"Alright then. Get off after his ass so I can sleep." She patted his back gently as he turned to go. It was reassuring, like something a grandmother might do. As he went back down the path towards his truck, he heard the screen door snap closed, then the softer sound of the inner one shutting.

He went to the passenger side and got the flashlight from the glovebox, giving it a quick check to make sure it worked. A high keening voice issued up behind him, distant. He turned and looked across the rows of levees, water high among the stalks of rice. At the edges of the field, there were pockets of trees interspersed with gaps where the lumber had been cut away. In one of those open spaces, he detected movement far across. A lanky form leapt over the levee into the dark screen of trees. He knew it was John, had to be. Even so, his heart made a little jump in his chest. *Goddamit, John, make it easy for me at least.*

He went down to the edge of the lawn and shone the flashlight around in the muddy water. One had to be wary of snakes, but perhaps it had gotten too cold for them. He stepped into the water and felt his boots sink into the mud.

A dog barked far off in the distance, the same direction he could just barely hear John's tearing voice over the ever-present sound of cicadas. Steady cloud cover was getting in the way of an already thin moon, visibility was low. He trod out, bouncing the light beam back and forth between his trajectory and his target. The voice was echoing among the far trees, the sound ragged and raw. His neck itched. Something in the night was bothering him; he just couldn't quite put his finger on what. Late, he realized the usual sound of buzzing insects had fallen away.

He had meant to holster the pistol in the back of his jeans but realized as he was a third of the way across the field that he still gripped it tight at his side. His face felt clammy, or maybe that was just the cold night air.

Just scare him off, get the dog, get back home. That's all. Don't make it more difficult than it needs to be.

The mud pulled harder each time he dragged a boot free. He was breathing jaggedly against the effort of wading through nearly knee high water. He cussed himself under his breath for letting his physicality slacken, if only for rare moments like this.

The voice fell silent for a while and Dan stopped to listen and catch his breath. He was close enough to the trees that his light beam could reach the trunks, but there was no sign of John or the dog. In the ensuing quiet, he became suddenly aware of a sound, an odd buzzing hum that made his hairs stand on end. It was so faint that he couldn't be sure he wasn't imagining it, but loud enough to draw his gaze skyward. Only a little fragment of moon peeked through the clouds as he scanned the pale-shaded void. His eyes aimlessly roved over the sky, then darted back as he registered something.

Reversed movement in the cloud layers.

Against the wind.

As he looked through the clouds, searching for the outline again, he heard something splash in the water. He jerked towards the wood and saw a low, four-legged shape come walking along the levee's crest toward him.

Wesley.

The stout German Shepherd passed him meekly, cutting its eyes at him in the light beam. Dan saw the fur hanging in wet strips from his belly, dripping where it had touched the levee water. A patch of fur around his neck was sticking out in all directions, matted with something. *Is that blood? Sonofabitch musta stabbed Wesley. Alright John, this is just too damn far.* He patted his leg and made noises at the dog, trying to get him to come over, but Wesley only glanced back briefly and kept going back toward the house.

Dan wanted a better look, the wounds didn't seem right, ringed around Wesley's neck like that. Almost could've been bites, as if the dog had been fighting an animal. He watched Wesley going farther out of his sight. The crawling feeling that something was very wrong tonight hit him again. *Awful calm for just getting cut on the neck ain't he?*

Something rustled in the leaves of the trees just ahead. He straightened quickly, shining the flashlight into it, searching for movement. Another rustle came, yards to the right of where he was just looking.

"John? Better come out of there, John, you've got everybody scared half to death." He adjusted his grip on the pistol, palms sweaty. He suddenly worried, what if John did come out? What would an addled or drunk man make of the sight of him with a gun? He held the pistol back behind his leg to hide it somewhat. The quiet moment slowly grew longer. The wood was silent, the sky was silent, and the field was silent, save for that low hum. He felt a flash of irritation, anger even. Dan wasn't used to being scared, especially on the account of some drunk like John Hadley. He didn't deserve to be out here chasing lunatics through a cold, flooded rice field, and his anger was helping convince him that was what was happening here. "John, that's enough of that. Get on out here, and let's get you home."

He passed the light over a thicket of bushes and then back again, thinking he saw eyes glint against the beam for a moment. The brush shifted in the breeze, hiding what he thought he'd seen. A wind was blowing up, building in intensity. He could feel it, but not its direction. It seemed to be coming from all around him, like a tornado that had just dropped out of the sky. The harsh wind whipped the bushes violently. The trees bucked and shuddered and the water shivered, and the light on them ran strangely yellow.

The bushes shattered with sudden movement as a man came sprinting out towards him.

Dan stepped back and brought the pistol up alongside the flashlight, aiming out of instinct, earlier ideas of what John would think forgotten. He registered that it was, in fact, John Hadley, the man's heavy black beard and bald head immediately recognizable. A new-looking esoteric tattoo ran around the top of one ear. John leapt from the edge of the water to the levee, slowing for a split second as his bare feet sunk into the mud. Then he broke free, barrelling sloppily through the knee-deep water towards Dan. In these small seconds, Dan saw John naked but for his boxers, but even more bizarre was the tattoo of an enormous cog on his chest over his heart. THis eyes were red and wild; his flesh was taut against his thin frame and strained with the rage of his action. John screamed, voice tearing against the beating he had been giving it all night, hoarse and terrified.

"RUN! THEY COMING!"

Dan would have shot him then and there had he not registered those words. Those three simple, perplexing words had stayed Dan's hand. It would have been a mercy.

The bushes John had broken from erupted again, a dark shape hurtling out into the water almost too fast for Dan to see. The water shattered into waves where it landed, churning around its path as it neared. Dan jerked his pistol towards the water, shouting wordlessly at the top of his lungs. John was only a couple of yards away when the thing emerged.

It moved faster than anything living he'd ever seen, writhing and coiling. It was long, maybe twice his height in length, and wormlike. It caught John Hadley a yard away from Dan, wrapping around his ribs and arcing over the levee with him into the water on the other side. Droplets of water side-slung off its body peppered his face like birdshot.

Dan lurched back and fell. He submerged, taking in a mouthful of disgusting brown water and losing his grip on his flashlight as his hands sought purchase in the mud. The muddy water ran into his eyes and coated his face, blinding him. He broke the surface, sputtering.

He might not have been able to see what the worm was doing to John beyond the levee, but he could hear it. If John was screaming, he couldn't hear it through the thrashing and splashing sounds. He could almost feel the filthy water choking John's voice away, crawling deeper and deeper down his throat as he drowned. Still seated, he raised the pistol up and shook it out, hoping the water hadn't clogged the barrel. He broke the cylinder again briefly, trying his best to ignore the horrible sounds on the other side of the levee, then closed the gun again and aimed it forward.

The thrashing stopped. He waited, listening. The wind had died as suddenly as it had come. His breath was like a scream to him, like a crop duster's engine roaring to life.

The worm-thing raised itself up, at once both elegant and hideous, towering over the levee. The way it moved made his hair stand on end, its feigned unearthly grace making him sick to watch after the violence with which it had gone after John. He could only know it in human terms as a worm, though it was plainly something else altogether. Its features were all ink-black against the thin moonlight, but he was sure it was looking right at him. Watching him the way a snake might watch a mouse who had wandered too close.

Please work.

He pulled the trigger and the pistol kicked in his hand with a sharp report. The worm jerked from the impact and lunged. He fired again and again, emptying all six bullets at it. His aim was good. He had been hunting since he was twelve, though not with revolvers. A remarkable cool had taken hold in his gun arm even as it had fled every other part of his body.

Heavy gunk splattered his face, but he blinked it away and held his aim. The worm reeled, screaming shrilly, and collapsed against the levee. Some of the moonlight hit the side of its head, and he registered multiple eyes with a segmented, sharp appendage anchored behind. Echoes of a centipede, or some other slithering insectoid. Heavy spasms rocked its body for several minutes before it finally fell still.

He splashed water in his face and wiped away the stuff, the blood from the thing, not thinking to inspect it first. His legs didn't want to work properly, he couldn't find it in him to stand. Instead, he half-crawled, half-swam over to the levee, and pulled himself up its side. The cloud cover had broken, and moonlight bathed the field for him to see what was left of John bobbing in the water a few feet past the worm.

In the corner of his eye, he registered movement distantly.

On the levee beyond the next, a distance of several dozen yards, he saw a gangly shape straddling the ridge of dirt and mud, watching. It was all black against the moonlight just like the worm had been with spindly arms draped off its narrow torso like branches, far too long to belong to a person. Dan froze, holding his breath, all too aware he was out of bullets. It studied the scene for a long time, then slid smoothly off into the water.

Dan pushed back off the levee as calmly as he could, which was not at all. He slipped low into the water and paddled back among the rice, putting as many yards between him and where he had been hiding as possible. He could hear the splashes of the alien; it must be an alien, no other word for it, as it came through the water towards him. Dan cowered as low as he could in the mud, only his face breaking the surface of the water. He let go of the empty gun, his hands wrapping around the underwater shafts of rice to hold his position as the alien mounted the ridge.

It crouched low on the levee and scanned the rice carefully. Its head turned mechanically as it did and he wondered if it didn't have the same wide field of vision people did. Though its head lined up with his position several times, it never betrayed recognition of him. Satisfied, it looked to the clouds. There was something in its hand, some device, and it raised it to the sky and emitted a harsh neon blue light.

Dan realized that the hum he had noticed before was rising in volume. A wind kicked up again, less intense than before, but still setting the trees to dancing and the water rippling softly. Something broke from the clouds above, dark and round and enormous. As he watched, the strange machine stopped, impossibly holding its position in midair. Cracks of light formed in the belly of the thing, metal crescents retracting like the aperture of a camera. A beam burned down to the earth from the glowing opening, falling across the bodies of the worm-thing and John Hadley. The alien stretched itself, raising its long vine-like arms to the sky, smaller offshoot limbs revealing and spreading from the main trunks like roots.

A pulsing whir joined the hum of the ship. The two corpses began to rise seemingly of their own accord. Dan watched in horrified awe as the bodies floated up, levitating higher and higher in the ship's beam, accompanied by weightless drops of blood and clods of dirt. They drifted closer together as they neared the apex of the beam, rotating slowly in the circle of light until they seemed one entwined creature. Abruptly, they disappeared into the belly of the thing and the metal crescents extended and locked back into place. The light winked out with a frightening finality.

The ship swept into smooth flight back up into the clouds, gone in moments. The alien stayed there for a few more minutes, passing its gaze over the rice with a final suspicion until it stepped quietly, carefully, along the crest of the levee like a woman going in the night. He watched it go with strange loping strides until it was lost among the far trees. Dan lay there for minutes on end, frozen with fear that the thing would come back for him if he betrayed his position. Perhaps as long as an hour later, the distant barking of a dog broke him from his terror. He rose shakily, tremoring in the cold with near-hypothermia, and began the walk back to Norma's.

The lights were on in the house when he emerged from the field and he saw Norma's silhouette move from the door. She came out the door, calling something to him but he was beyond listening. Wesley stopped barking when it saw him, but his head was down and wary and he didn't approach. Dan got into his truck without saying a single word and drove home.

———

DAN SITS at the dining table, which he has not used for a proper meal in half a year. He looks out the window that faces the rice fields. It's night, and he has watched every night to see if they will come back. Part of it is to prove that what he saw that night was real. John Hadley has never resurfaced. His neighbors have raised concerns about the eccentric's absence. Some have even said that Dan killed him that night among the levees. Some days, Dan wonders if they're right.

He keeps his rifle cleaned and loaded and laid out across the table, and a pistol under his pillow. Norma no longer calls. He wonders if they will try to take him. Queerly, he thinks it would be nice to be wanted.

RIVER SONG

THERE ARE MEN IN THE YARD.

Anna watched from up the gravel driveway, her hands locked on the steering wheel at nine and three o'clock. Her breath hissed through the tiny slit of her lips, and her eyebrows knitted into an arrowhead aiming down the bridge of her nose. There were at least a dozen of them tossing a football back and forth on the dying autumn grass. Worse, they had crossed over the driveway separating the two cabins to her side, her space. Or at least two of them had, uncaring of the clear dividing line. The headlights cast shadows from the trees far among them and the men leapt agilely in and out of them in their game.

She sat in her car, hands lightly trembling. She wasn't far from them or the cabins, maybe fifty feet, and beams were unignorable in the fading dusk. Should she just leave? She contemplated it, though that meant having to reverse her way back half a mile on the snaking, narrow road. A lull in the game had come now, and several of them were looking her way. Now seen and too self-conscious to retreat, Anna clenched her teeth and started up the drive.

No kind of courage, but something that resembled it in the right absence of light.

Headlights shining, she advanced slowly through them, some backing off the gravel to the grass to either side. She hoped the lights temporarily blinded them and left echoing, indistinguishable shapes in their eyes. They wouldn't see her enter the cabin then. She parked among the thick, round stilts below the building and watched the men in her yard cross back over to their's sheepishly. When she got out and started up the stairs, one of them called out something to her in an unfamiliar accent. Anna climbed faster, unlocking the door and closing it firmly behind her.

Mrow.

The cat called to her when she came through the door, padding over to her across the wooden floor on fat feet. The cat could not sneak up on a mouse, but for all its clumsiness there was little it could not destroy when its mind was set on it. They had never decided on a good name. It had always felt like they were merely passing by one another. She stooped and scratched its head before walking through the kitchen and into the bedroom. The comfortable chair in the corner was almost always her first stop when she returned to the cabin. It was perfect, just the right size for curling up with a good book, or occasionally peeking out the perennially drawn shutters at what was happening outside. The large bedroom window covered nearly the entire wall while overlooking both the river and the nearby cabins, and Anna used it to keep abreast of the comings and goings of the neighboring vacationers. She stood by that soft, inviting chair and parted two layers of the cheap shutters with thumb and forefinger to peek out. They were proceeding as they had been, laughing and throwing a ball, not looking up at her. The light from their cabin didn't reach fully to their field of play and they streaked, dark and featureless, between the trees now without the illumination of her car.

Anna knew she shouldn't be so discomforted by a large group of strangers nearby. The cabin next door was a rental, after all. In the summer there was someone new every week, but this late in the season the stream of customers had slowed to a trickle. For her, each surprise neighbor was only a new pulse of dread inside. She felt flanked. She picked up the phone.

Her mother answered on what felt like the very last ring before it went to voicemail.

"Hi, honey!"

"There's men outside."

"What do you mean?"

"There's a bunch of men next door. They were in my yard."

"Oh. Well they're just tourists right? Did they do something?"

"No, besides being in my yard for a little bit. They moved back over."

"Okay, well, what's the problem then?"

"I don't know . . . I guess I'm not used to it being all men next door. I didn't see one woman. And there's so many of them."

"Did they say something?"

"Well one did, I think. But he sounded foreign."

She paused and Anna heard her saying something to someone else. She could imagine her standing there with the phone pressed into the shirt at her shoulder. "Your brother says you're being racist." She laughed.

"I'm not scared because they're foreign, I was just mentioning it."

"Sure, sure. Look honey, it'll be fine, just keep the doors locked. They'll mind their own business."

Anna walked away from the window as they talked of normal things. Things they had to do, who her mother had bumped into in town, or what the weather was supposed to do next week. When they were done, it was full dark. She laid the phone down and tried to relax the tension in her shoulders, letting out a long, coiled breath into the quiet.

She heard distant laughter, slipping through some weakness in the walls to break her peace. She went back to the window. The wooded yard had stilled. She went back out and into the kitchen and through the window there saw that the interlopers had moved to the elevated deck. They stood in packs armed with beer cans, illuminated brightly, observing the oil-dark waters below drift by. Music pulsed out in waves from somewhere without definition.

Fears assuaged, she slumped on the couch and scrolled aimlessly through streaming apps looking for an appetizing movie. The cat curled beside her, gently kneading her leg with its claws. She slipped away into sleep.

It was deep in the night when she woke again, long enough that the TV had powered down automatically. She didn't move for many long minutes, studying the patterned shadows across the ceiling. A low yellow glow invaded the space, setting those shadows to flight. The couch she sat on was arranged against the wall beside the balcony facing the river. The curtains were pulled, that was where the light was coming. Turning her head, she saw the cat settled into a loaf on the neck rest of the love seat, looking through the glass where the light was coming through. Its eyes were big black saucers, and they did not blink.

She shakily rose and went to the glass and looked out. A boat was coming down the river, amber light beaming out from the front and sides beneath the water brilliantly. The dazzling light illuminated three men, one at the wheel and two forward. A lantern hung from a hook above them, an open cooler stacked with ice and beer cans below it. She saw gigging spears in their hands, poised for a thrust into the dark waters.

There was something in the light, some longing that drew her like she was one of the poor fish they hunted. Weak-willed and base in desire, pulled to the light and worthy of slaughter. She wondered how she must look to them, had they glanced high for a moment. Just some girl watching strangely with burning, golden eyes. She wanted to bathe in its beauty, to risk the slaughter. To be vulnerable, for once in her life, unafraid. She blinked and ripped her gaze away, looking across to the opposite bank. Something pulled her attention to the tall hill on the other side of the river. Lights had come on in the house that sat high up on its side. She thought she could barely see a person standing out on the deck, watching as she did.

What do you want, she thought, then turned the question inward. A shiver wracked her body despite the house's warmth.

When she looked again to the fishermen, she saw that there was something trailing behind them in the water.

In no world could it have been mistaken for a fish, a man-sized mass of shimmering silver that followed gracefully in the wake of the boat like a shark. The fishermen stood further up in the boat, looking forward with their lances couched. There was never going to be the hint of a thought to look behind. The silver thing seemed to know where the men were focused, drifting along at the edge of the light behind the boat. Anna watched transfixed as the light reflected from it, layers of it shifting around it like the folds of a gown. For a split-second, it overshot its positioning and slid farther into the light than it had been, and a woman's face sprouted into sight, fae and ethereal with long hair that fanned out behind her like a cape in the water.

Anna's breath caught as she pressed a palm to the glass. She tried to get a better look at her face, but the woman in the water disappeared as suddenly as she had come. Frantic now, Anna stared into the sickly, green deep, waiting for her to return. But the boatmen floated on, and she could only watch until they were out of sight. She wondered if she had gone mad. Was this a dream? Had she never woken up and would know the truth in just a moment when the sweet, terrifying veil lifted? She looked up and saw that far up on the opposite hill that stranger still stood on the deck. She wondered if they had been waiting there to see the woman in the water all along. Maybe they were standing there wondering if they were still sane, just like she was.

Anna never woke up.

She wasted much of the next day with menial chores and aimless entertainment, the woman in the water haunting her every moment. She yearned for night to fall, to see if the boat would pass by again and give her a glimpse below the surface. The sun beamed down on her powerfully, yet it seemed pathetic next to that glow in the dark. Context could be an overwhelming thing. A burning star unfathomably distant, a fixture in her world, and yet now it held no allure. Against the darkness something as mundane as the lights of a boat held divinity. She tried to squint into the shadow of the sun. She was sure it was hiding nothing, only pretending to have treasures.

Anna sat on the small dock below the cabin, stripped her shoes and socks off and dangled her toes in the water. Snakes sunbathed on the rock slopes to either side, but she only had eyes for the water. *Come out and say hello.*

"Hello," a man's voice said.

She flinched and dug her fingers into the wood of the dock as she looked back. The man leaned on one of the posts at the top of the stairs, smiling. He was tan with dark hair and eyes. Probably handsome in the eyes of most. Fit, capable.

"How is the water?" he asked. He had an accent, but not a strong one.

"You're on my property."

"Oh. I'm sorry." He stood straight, smile flickering but not vanishing. He left his hand on the post. He knew it was her property. The dock extended directly out in front of the cabin. It was obvious, but he had come anyway. "I meant no offense."

She heard her mother's voice somewhere, telling her not to be rude. "It's ok, no big deal." She stood up and turned to him, but didn't approach. He wasn't threatening, but still she was conscious that he was blocking her only path off the dock that wasn't into the water.

"You sound very American. A little country," he said, laughing.

"You don't."

"I am, actually. American, that is. From when I was a little boy. My parents came from Turkey, as did my cousins." He gestured to the men who were out in the yard next door. Some were watching.

"You have a lot of cousins."

"I do. Some of them wondered if you would join us for lunch. We are grilling burgers and hot dogs."

"I'm fine, thank you."

"You're sure? It's your last chance, we will be leaving in a few hours."

"I'm sure, thank you."

"As you say then. Have a nice day."

When he was gone, she sat down against one of the

posts and faced the stairs to make sure he didn't sneak up on her again while she called her mother.

"Hi, honey."

"Hi."

She must have heard the tone in Anna's voice, even on that one tiny syllable. "What's wrong?"

Anna told her. At the end of it, she said, "It's not right for him to barge into my space like that. It's mine. It's obvious that it's mine."

"I know, but it's not like he came into the house uninvited. He meant well."

"I deserve privacy."

"Well, put up a fence."

She answered with a sullen silence.

"You've got bigger things to worry about. Focus on the future." Anna let the issue go, or at least stopped arguing about it. She listened to her mother talk for a while about nothing. By mid-afternoon the men had left, having piled into dusted rental cars and gone. By then, being alone didn't make Anna feel any better.

Night fell again, and the TV flashed violently in the dark room. Anna sat on the arm of the couch looking through the glass at the river. Hours passed before a pale glow swelled far up the current. She stood abruptly, hurriedly shoving the door out of the way as she stepped onto the balcony.

She couldn't see the boat yet. The amber was washing over and through the gaps in the branches of the trees on the river's flanks, but they were dense enough to block the source. She ran a hand along the wooden railing absently, waiting, and threw a glance at the high cabin. One single light was on, but no one was on the deck. Her gaze fell and, with a start, she saw the neighbor standing on the gravel beach below in her robe. Anna had never seen the woman leave her house before, but here she was. The woman's eyes watched the nearing glow implacably.

The cat chittered, slipping through the door she had left ajar. Having made its escape, the pesky animal jumped up onto the railing, walking over to her in the self-satisfied way cats do. Making a shooing noise, Anna drove the cat back indoors, ducking slightly at it and fluttering her hands. The beast retreated and she shut the door behind it. Looking back, she saw that the boat had come into view.

Capsized.

A flush of night wind passed over her like a ghost. The light was beaming even more powerfully outside the water from the upturned hull, yet it had lost its luster in this new, sinister context. It no longer magicked her as it had before; its shine muted as it passed through the lens of water. Anna gasped and clasped a hand to her mouth as if someone might hear her. Her other hand gripped the railing until it hurt. No one was swimming in the water; no bodies floated past. *The fishermen could've swam to shore upriver if their boat flipped. Stop freaking out.* But it was hard to imagine what had flipped a boat that size. Anna couldn't recall ever having seen a jonboat flip, and this one was nearly 14 feet long with a deep keel, larger and heavier than most of its kind.

Anna watched helplessly as the boat streamed past and around the next bend. She had just turned to go back inside when she heard it. A tune, a melody. Music of a kind she had never heard before. The notes swelled and rose, blending and tumbling together in a flow so beautiful that she couldn't help but turn to see its source. She looked back to see her strange neighbor on the beach, staring out into the center of the current. And there, in the middle of the swiftly rolling water, was a person. Anna could see their head and the top of their shoulders, almost as if they were standing on something below the surface. Their hair might have been any color but was an inky black in the dark, the skin of their shoulders gleaming palely in the wet moonlight. The song was a high falsetto and wordless, so proud and pure in its notes. Tears ran down Anna's face as she listened. Why wouldn't the woman in the water look at her? Her mind fogged. She wanted to get closer. The woman on the beach took stilted steps down toward the water's edge. Anna's vision blurred. She couldn't make out anything more than the neighbor's white bathrobe bunching and floating up around her as the water came· up to her middle.

Anna took a step across the balcony, trying to near in whatever tiny way she could, but she had to grab the railing with both hands to steady herself when the first step slipped. The song raged both in and outside of her head. Her vision faded and she collapsed.

It was past dawn when she woke, well into the morning with the sun burning down on her aching body. She lay there for a long time. Through the slit between the railing and the balcony floor she scanned the far beach without even having to lift her head. A deer had come down to drink, but no woman. She rolled over and saw the cat watching her through the glass. It rose up on its hind legs and pawed for her. She rose and went inside.

She left the news on throughout the day until the story about the three missing fishermen came up. The anchors all said it was exceedingly odd to have found no trace of them except for the capsized boat, given how many cabins sat along the river, not to mention the nearby put-in points for floaters. Foul play was suspected. She found a phone number for the cabin on the opposite hill and called at regular intervals through the afternoon to no answer. Dusk came and still no light blinked on from that lonely height.

Anna's mother called. She watched it ring for a few seconds, then let it go to voicemail.

Anna sat quietly on the couch. She had been sitting there for hours, thinking and building her resolve. A half-finished bottle of wine sat on the floor beside her with no glass. She resolved herself to something both terrifying and exhilarating. People had gone missing after all, and somehow, that woman was involved. But when Anna thought about this, all she could remember was the song. It wasn't just that the song was beautiful, though beautiful even seemed a meager word for it. It was what it did to her. The notes pulled at her, raising old memories and easing her anxieties in just the right way. They were warm, like a hug from someone who loved you unconditionally. Someone who saw you. Someone who would never hurt you, because of that knowing. She straightened and neatened everything in the house, made the bed, folded the blanket on the couch. Night neared slowly.

When all the orange had gone out of the horizon, Anna went resolutely down to the dock. She wondered why she didn't feel afraid anymore. It was hard to imagine a time in which she hadn't been. She looked up the river, then down it, then deep into the depths at her feet. Waiting. She waited a long time, but the woman in the water didn't come. She scuffed her bare feet against the wood, sat and waved them in the water, knocked on the post with her nails. Anna would see the woman again. She would wait all night if she had to. The dock elbowed at the foot of the slope along the rocks where the snakes sunbathed, and she paced from one end to the other. On one pass, something caught her eye among the posts below the dock's stair, something hung up among the rocks.

She felt the chill keenly, looking at that strange too-large and too-oval shape blackly silhouetted under there.

Secreted like treasure beneath a bridge. Her hands shook as she produced her phone and pressed the flashlight function. It didn't beam like one, but rather swept out widely and the light was sterile and unnerving no matter the subject.

Two mossy green eyes caught the light first, staring out of the pale, decapitated head of a woman.

The shadows closed back over their prize hungrily as she dropped the phone. She dropped to a crouch and clumsily pried it off the flat surface it seemed to have suctioned to. Turning it over in her hands and flashing that enormous, plastic light around felt like turning herself into a lighthouse for a few terrifying moments. She sat on her knees and steadied her breathing. One thought. *It can't stay here.*

It couldn't. The lonely river house didn't deserve to be the site at which a murdered woman's head was discovered. This was not a place for police to visit, to carry it away and identify it for a family somewhere in a cold morgue, for the woods to be bathed in flashing red and blue lights. It was all an accident anyway. The woman in the water hadn't meant for this. It was chance that this head had washed up here. All it required was a little nudge and the site would move possibly miles downstream and the woman would know it was safe.

The head was under the stairs. She went around the elbow of the dock's design and knelt down over the edge of it on the lower step, shining the light down at it. The hair had plastered across the scalp when wet, but now was going dry and stringy and brittle. She had to work to twine enough strands together to hold, but eventually she drew it up into the moonlight. She stood and stepped down on the flat of the dock, looking down at the head dangling from her grip by the hair like a bag of groceries.

She looked down at the end of the dock, and there she was. The woman from the water.

Anna swore there was a glow coming off her, off her skin. A pale and trembling silver that drifted off her in waves. Like there was so much beauty in her that its excess had to slough off and be shared. The woman had laid her arms one atop the other on the wood and then her chin atop that, watching Anna's sin. And she smiled. Oh how she smiled. Like she loved it, loved the illicit secret in it, loved being privy to it. But that it would be safe with her too. The intimacy of knowing one another's skeletons.

The woman lifted her head and her mouth gently opened as if to speak. Only a moment of that first note of song issued before Anna knew what was happening, and knew she had to act or the moment would be lost forever. She wound her arm back and flung the head, spinning, out into the center of the water. It bobbed and rolled with the current until out of sight. The woman had stopped her song immediately and turned to watch it go, then looked at Anna intently.

Anna carefully turned the phone off and set it on the middle step behind her. Then she approached.

THE PEOPLE IN THE FORT

I.

CALEB WATCHED AUTUMN TREES DASH BY THROUGH THE truck window, an old honky-tonk song blaring from the front. His grandparents were hard of hearing and had turned the radio way too loud, so loud that he could hear it even with his headphones on at full volume. After a few minutes of trying to ignore the deafening sounds of jangling blue steel guitars, he gave up and laid his now useless headphones next to him in the backseat. The irony was not lost on him that the "old people's music", as he thought of it, was drowning out the heavy metal he'd been trying to listen to. His funeral clothes sat strangely on his body and had him shifting uncomfortably at each country mile passed. A new song kicked on, and he groaned inwardly as he heard Grandpa say, "Hey, turn that up. That's a good 'un."

They turned into the gravel driveway that climbed for a quarter of a mile up the side of the cattle-dotted hill, taking a hard right turn as the road led them to the old house. A few sheet metal barns guarded one side and a tree-speckled yard held the other three. They parked outside under a rain guard, then went inside to change. Grandpa settled down into his old chair with the quilt he always had draped across it tucked snugly down into the cracks. He leaned back for a nap, the TV playing Gunsmoke reruns. Grandma disappeared into their bedroom for a quieter nap. He keenly felt the interior temperature in his stuffy funeral clothes, always set too hot for his taste.

He went to the spare bedroom to change, tight fists in his pockets. The room was his, but not *his*. Little in it reflected him. The quilt on the bed was flowery and home-spun and out of fashion like the ones in his grandparent's room. The closet was three quarters empty, barely filled by what few clothes he still owned. Most of these weren't really his either; either old hand-me-downs or charity. A box of action figures sat in there with them, absorbing dust. There was an acoustic guitar in the corner, the highest string missing. There was a smell in the room, like in the rest of the house, that he could only describe as a grandparent smell.

He put on his dirty sneakers, an Iron Maiden T-shirt, old jeans ripped from use rather than design like some of the kids at school wore, and a dark denim coat and went outside. A black mutt, splotched with white, parked itself at his feet and looked up at him expectantly. *Walk?* its eyes asked. He crossed the yard and started trekking back down the eighth-mile of driveway toward the corner where the forest began, then followed it the rest of the way down to the county road. The mutt bounded through the field to his right, sending a few calves lurching towards their mothers. Caleb liked the woods, especially that time of year with the leaves in color and the air cooling down ahead of winter. And it was quiet there, no people.

He was thinking while he walked. He liked thinking, usually. It was like dreaming awake. He thought about the pile of smoldering, blackened timbers and the boy that settled down cross-legged on the concrete walk that led to the porch that no longer existed. The concrete was so cold when he sat down, but his face was flushed. He'd forgotten his gameboy inside and thought of it. A neighborhood cat prowled over and rubbed itself against the boy, uninterested in the destruction. The fire truck sirens screamed down the street.

The dog growled a warning.

He looked up and saw the dog whose name he hadn't bothered to learn. It stood at the line where the road ended against the shallow ditch separating it from the trees, a moat guarding a castle it dared not approach. A squat square structure of wooden boards, maybe six feet in height, stood among the trees just a few feet past the ditch, roofless with the walls going to rot. Several boards, shaded with light splotches of mossy green, had fallen away over the years since his father and uncle had built what they had called "The Fort". It had been a project for he and his cousins, his father purchasing them the pieces to construct their playplace in the hopes that it would teach them something about hard work when chased down by desire. They had given up before they got to the roof, but it had served them well for a time with their imaginations filling in the places their resolve and work ethics had failed. There was a little square port in the front wall, a gun or arrow hole in their minds. They played soldier there, cowboys and indians, cops and robbers.

Two figures stood among the collapsing planks. They were indistinct, impossible to grasp any features aside from the hazy outlines or the eyes that glowed yellow like flashlights. One of them seemed vaguely feminine, but it was hard to tell for sure. They were the exact same height, a fact which registered with him distantly. Only their outline from the chest up was visible over the front wall of the fort. They stood, motionless, watching.

The dog whimpered and trotted past him back towards the old house. He followed and didn't look back.

II.

Caleb and his grandpa sat in the grass watching birds flit around the big oak tree in the yard. They leaned .22 rifles against their shoulders, occasionally blowing into their hands for warmth.

"Hard ain't it?"

Caleb didn't say anything.

"My Ma died of cancer when I was twenty. That's different from bein' your age, but it still ain't no good. You'll be in college by that time. I weren't. It was the farm for me."

The wind began to whistle.

"If you wanna talk about it, lemme know. Don't know that it helps none. Some says it does. You just bear it, mostly."

Some birds landed on the electric wire just beyond the tree in clear view of them.

"Take a shot at one of them, why don't ya."

Caleb lifted the rifle, aimed it, and fired. A bird dropped off the wire and bounced off the wooden fence. One second, it was there squabbling and preening with the others, and then just gone. The crack of the gun didn't even leave his ears ringing, it wasn't powerful enough. The other birds lit off to another site or fluttered around the top of the tree again.

He used to get a little thrill every time he plugged one. Now he felt nothing. He leaned the rifle against his shoulder and began blowing into his cupped fingers again, watching them fly.

III.

Caleb dreamt of them in the night, hazy walking shadows with flashlight eyes. In the dream, it was a moonlit night; this time, Caleb walked right past them toward the end of the drive, going out to the county road beyond. When he turned to look back, he saw that they were following him. Not sprinting after him or chasing him, just walking. It might have even been his exact pace. He never stopped walking himself, but frequently looked back over his shoulder and found them about the same distance behind, perfectly side by side, their steps in sync. The dream ended at the county road, like most things in this kind of country. When he stopped there, he turned to look back and saw that they hadn't.

Early the next morning, he went out again. The lingering night chill raked him, and he balled up his fists in the pockets of his jacket and tucked his chin down into his collar. The dog fell down onto its belly by a tree at the end of the yard and would not follow him further. It watched him go with sad eyes, whining.

He stared straight ahead the whole walk down to the corner, searching, seeking them, but found the fort empty. He stepped over the ditch into the forest, thinking perhaps that there was a magical property to the boundary line that might trip some spectral happening. When nothing came of it, he breathed a sigh of relief. Instead of walking from there down to the county road, as was his routine, he wandered aimlessly around the fort, sometimes leaning against it, his headphones pounding Mayhem into his skull. He liked the early demos, especially Pure Fucking Armageddon. There was something hard in it, yet also something a little brittle.

He returned to the old house before lunch and spent the day in his room, skimming books full of wartime photographs from the second world war. American war history was an interest of his grandfather, who had never served except in peacetime.

Caleb was being left to himself most of the time, but it would end eventually. A return to school loomed, a return to normalcy. He wasn't ready.

Late in the afternoon, almost dusk, he went outside again. The heat inside had gotten to him and he wanted cool air. He hadn't meant to venture beyond the yard, but when he got outside, a glow caught his eye over the distant tree tops beyond the fort. The dog again refused to set foot past the end of the yard as he passed. He watched for the specters through his approach, but nothing appeared to greet him. At the ditch he stopped and stared into the deepening gloom between shedding red and yellow elms and evergreen pines. A clutch of the evergreens beyond the fort blocked out his view, but a hint of glow reached through down around their trunks. He looked westward at the setting sun for a moment, then stepped across the ditch, past the little fort, and finally up to the tiny stray strand of barbed wire that hovered an inch off the ground between two trees, the one that served to mark the start of the true woods. He had more than once wondered where that had come from. He sensed a finality as he stepped over.

He had to duck among the low, dense branches that

grew close over his path. Something leapt in the brush to his side, but he barely noticed. He followed the light.

Caleb knew something was wrong when he came into the clearing. He had been there before. The last time he'd come to stay with his grandparents for a weekend, he'd walked every inch of the wood. By memory, he knew there should have been nothing there, nothing but a place for deer to come out of hiding, if one were quiet.

Instead, there was another fort.

Not a half-finished structure of wood that had been falling away for years, decades. Not a remnant of another person's childhood, forgotten. A real fort.

It had stone walls that reached high to heaven, tall as the trees surrounding it. Lit torches were sconced here and there, one to either side of a gate twice his height. The doors were thick and thrown wide. Fires danced along the medieval-styled ramparts, a flag whose sigil was obscured to him blowing with the wind atop a tower at one corner.

He approached the gate, cautious like a mouse going watchful through the grass for fear of a hawk. Nothing sprang from the shadows, no noises greeted him. He went through the gate into a courtyard well-lit with torches on every wall. His outline danced against the stones as he moved, larger than he was in real life. A stone keep sat opposite the gate he had come through, colossal and imposing. He had read a fantasy book once with knights and kings and monsters and there was a scene where the heroes were backed into the inner keep of a castle just like this. Where they held out for days against a horde of evil.

The doors to the keep creaked open, and forth came the walking shadows.

He froze there, wide-eyed, and watched as they approached him, their steps in perfect sync. Right foot, left foot, right foot, left foot, every step made by one mirrored by its companion. Their flashlight eyes burned into him. He felt their heat. There was still an indistinctness to them, but at that distance he was even more sure that one was feminine by the shape of its body and what may have been shoulder-length hair softly shifting around the outline of its head. It was like a haze of static existed around them, television static with a coating of black cigarette smoke. Their height was the same, loosely gendered doppelgangers of one united entity.

The man-shadow reached out to touch him with its dark, shifting arm. The woman-shadow diverged from its partner and stood still there beside and watched. He flinched and began backing away to the gate, checking once over his shoulder to make sure more shadows hadn't appeared behind him. When he looked back to the two, he saw that they were following him but only slowly, with strangely tender steps. He backed through the gate into the woods, then turned and started walking straight towards the old, rotting fort and the gravel road. He checked behind himself twice on the way back, and both times found them on his trail with their bright beam eyes on his back. He made it to the road and halfway down it checked a third time to find that they had taken up their old post in the small fort, watching him go. He returned to the house and knelt by his bedroom window that looked over the road to watch for them. He didn't even notice that it was deep into the night by that point, hours till dawn.

IV.

They walked the woods to the north with their .22s, the opposite side of the property from the fort. The forest was quiet except for the heavy sound of their boots on the dry leaves. The dog loped out to the side. They heard small animals driven before it, but it was difficult to see them in the brush.

"You're gonna need school clothes, ain't ya?"

"I got some."

"Them jeans is pretty tore up. If it was my Ma dressing you she'd throw that shirt out too."

He glanced at his Slayer tee, one of three shirts that were actually his that had survived the fire. When he looked back up the foot-worn path he saw a gray animal smaller than a dog scuttling across. Without thinking, he lifted up the rifle and fired three times after it, but it bolted to safety.

"That was a cat, you don't wanna be shooting them."

"I'm tired of birds."

"Well . . . maybe we can get you started deer hunting next year. Big game." He smiled.

Caleb smiled back.

V.

Caleb dreamed he was in the oddly dim, dank catholic church again, the holy place where the priest was so old that he seemed less than human. A leering, groping ghoul whispering things into his ear that were probably meant to be comforting. People he didn't know or maybe barely knew patted his back and slipped away before he could respond to their comments. He sat in the front row, silent in his uncomfortable suit, and stared at the two closed caskets beneath the big cross. They weren't closed because the bodies were too disfigured to look upon, but because there were no bodies to display. *Ashes.* A picture of them from their wedding day stood on a little end table placed between the two caskets. His grandmother was hovering near it. "She was so tall," she said in that brittle, wavering voice of the grieving. "She went without heels on the day because she didn't want to be taller than him, make him feel inadequate. A kind soul she was, so thoughtful. Everything was for him."

A second dream came on, a briefer one he remembered well. He was outside the burnt house with the fire trucks screaming toward him. The fire was thoroughly finished by that point, so the firemen mostly stood around watching. He never knew why it had taken them so long to arrive. Out in the country, a fire was less likely to be reported in time to stop it, but it almost could not be missed in a suburb like this.

Caleb wasn't looking at anything except the black cloud that churned above the pile. It was so conspicuous and ominous, and yet none of the men noticed it. Someone eventually shuffled him into an ambulance. As it peeled away from the scene he stared out the back window at the dark shapes around his old home. Black smoke poured out onto the street behind him, and just before it all faded out of sight, twin pairs of flashlight eyes beamed out of two of the shapes, looking after him.

He sat up in bed, sweating, and looked out the window. The night outside was still fully dark. For a long while, he sat there, thoughts churning in his head. He went and got the guitar from the corner and plucked at the strings. He had been learning to play, but his electric guitar and amp were gone with the rest. He had learned a few riffs, but he had no pick to play with and it would never sound right coming from an acoustic guitar anyway. He tried, hammering on the low string with his thumb and trying to imagine it how it should be, the smoking, crackling distortion and the hum of the speakers cranked loud. It didn't work, would never work. A gasp tore from his throat and he threw the guitar across the room where it knocked against the dresser. The strings banged discordantly in the quiet house. He gritted his teeth against the scream and a groan ground through. He sat and listened for long minutes, tears streaking down his cheeks, but his grandparents were too hard of hearing and too deep in sleep to have noticed.

He slipped into his outdoor clothes again, going quietly through the house on his toes with two fingers hooked through the holes of his sneakers. In his pocket were two old lighters he had found in his bedroom closet. He had tested them both to make sure they worked and brought both in case one should fail. In the garage was a bright red 5-gallon gas can, mostly full, for fueling the lawnmower. He picked it up, on the way by grabbing a flashlight. The dog watched him go from the bundle-bed of old blankets and towels by the little plug-in heater they used in the cooler months.

Nothing shone from the forest on his approach. All was black. He flicked the flashlight's beam into the fields to either side and saw no more than the occasional black-furred cow. When he reached the end of the road he could see the faintest bit of light beginning to show on the horizon.

He climbed into the little fort through the open side and began dousing the boards with gas. He circled it, throwing up splashes of the stuff against the falling walls. Once, he glanced toward the vague path that he had followed to find the big fort, but nothing glowed through the gaps in between branches or at the open space by their roots. Finally, he knelt at one corner, drew a flame from the first lighter he chose, and touched it to the nearest wetness.

The little fort went up instantly, and he stepped back away from the sudden heat, watching. It would take a while to burn, he knew, but he had time. He would watch every inch of wood consumed and if there was some that endured beneath the ashes of the rest then he would dig through it all with a shovel and burn that to nothingness too.

He looked again deeper into the woods and saw that a glow had sprung up again, seeping through the trees. He followed the path, again, leaving the emptied gas jug behind. Dismay shot through him, wondering how he could burn down a fort of stone instead of wood.

When he came into the clearing, though, he found it burning of its own accord.

The fort of heavy stone and mortar, as it had stood when he had found his way to it earlier, was now engulfed in a flame of unnatural fury and power. Fire licked up the walls and over the ramparts, to the top of the turrets and the gatehouse, back down the stairs and across the ground to the inner keep. All was aflame. The heavy stones turned molten beneath the heat and dripped down into the raw earth. The intensity of the inferno splashed against his cheeks even fifty feet away, but he would not turn his gaze from the scene. He would see it through.

Atop the gatehouse stood the two shadows, watching him. He thought for several terrible minutes that they would endure even this and come for him again, forever, but they disintegrated beneath the fire too eventually, as their castle was brought low around them. Two insignificant wisps of smoke blown away by wind.

When he saw that they were gone, Caleb sat down and watched the fort burn for a while longer, a faint smile on his lips. When that too was done he lay back among the leaves and dirt and stared up at the sky, which had begun to lighten with the dawn.

THE NEEDLE

My home is a cube of harsh, gray stone. Perhaps it is not a perfect cube. I have not attempted to measure it in an immeasurable length of time, and I find it makes no difference to me now. The floor is stone, the walls are stone, the roof is stone. Unyielding, unpolished, faceless stone. The walls are adorned with a few paintings. I care for two of them. One depicts a wheatfield. There are a few trees along a distant fencerow, but the rest of it is golden wheat and blue sky. It looks warm, but not hot. The other depicts a family: a father, a mother, a son, and a daughter. There are four of us here in the cube, and we are family, but this painting is not of us. We do not resemble the people painted inside, and the composition is all wrong. Unlike the painting there is no father here, nor do I remember one. It is unclear to me which of us in the cube is the extra, me or my brother. The painted family is arranged in a line, staring morosely at me from outside a picturesque house. It looks like the sort of house that might have stood near the wheatfield, but I cannot be sure. Perhaps that is why I like it.

There is no door in the cube, nor even the outline of one. We cannot leave. There have been no attempts to defeat the obvious. There would be no point.

There are four beds, one for each of us. There is a desk with a chair, several pencils, and a stack of paper. These belong to my brother, for he is a writer. I do not know of what he writes and have never asked. My sister and my mother have similar spaces; their task is to paint, and so they sit before a stack of canvas arranged on an easel and paint the things that come to them. Purely by accident, I have glimpsed a few of their works; a bed with sheets tucked in and pillows fluffed, a chasm with a single point of brightness, the back of a child's head. I do not intentionally look, for I have my own task, and its name is music.

Beside my bed is a stack of records that stands taller than I do, and I am quite tall relative to my family. A record player sits on a small table beside the stack of records. Every morning, I use it to listen to one at random every morning for one hour. I have no choice in the length of my listening time, for the record player goes silent of its own accord when that hour is done. It does not seem to matter when that hour takes place; only once it begins will it not cease until that hour is done. I prefer to do it first thing in the morning. I have a violin and a case that it goes into when I am done playing, and of course, a bow to play with. Every day, when I have finished listening to whatever record was chosen, I play. I play while my brother writes and while my sister and mother paint. These are our tasks.

I had before wondered how each of us knew which task belonged to us when we woke unfettered in this gray, indomitable place, but now I feel that we just knew. My oldest memory is opening my eyes to the sight of that stone sky and the smell of something sour. Within a short amount of time, I had found the violin where it was hidden beneath the bed and explored it thoroughly. I do not think I was born here. But I remember nothing before, so in a way, it could be said that I was born here. My mother has no answers. She stopped answering my questions long ago. I no longer ask.

Of late, my nights are haunted with terrors where once I saw nothing but the peace of dark. Last night, I saw a creature wrapped in but pale shreds of cloth. It had a body like my mother's but a newborn child's face, so white and small and ungrazed. Its eyes were wide black orbs lacking pupil and iris, staring endlessly as it played my violin. The music it made was beautiful in a mournful way, sad and inevitable. Its eyes were ever on me as it played, but I could not move to take back what is mine, mine alone forever, always.

The night before, I saw small things that crawled over every inch of the cube and they touched me as I looked at them through slitted eyes. I think they did not know I could see them. They forced something down my throat and pulled up my shirt to do something that I could not see. I could not see the creatures well as I was looking at them in secret, but their blurry visages seemed pale and small. Above them, the stone ceiling was gone, and a giant eye looked down at us all. A normal eye but for its size, not the deep inky black of the woman-child-creature but a deep green, the green of the trees in my second favorite painting. It is the thing that haunts me most.

My usual routine is to choose a record different from the previous day, but thirty-seven times in a row I have found myself choosing the same one. It is simply called "Songs of Hill and Mountain" and neither songs nor singer are named. The case is unadorned, plain even, but for all that mystery it is a simple and lively collection of songs that bring me joy. There is an instrument in most of the songs that sounds very much like my violin and yet does not; it is so much more vibrant and energetic, and it distresses me greatly that my playing sounds so very wooden in comparison.

After many hours of playing, eventually, there comes a vibration in the stone. I have only come to notice it recently because it is such a slight thing I barely feel beneath my feet. Then comes a sweet smell that conjures the color yellow in my head, and we all become immediately very tired. We are so tired that we cannot help but to go to our beds and sleep until we wake.

And then it begins anew, with that same sour smell I smelled when first I awoke.

Then came a day that was wholly different. Once more I chose to listen to "Songs of Hill and Mountain". This marked the thirty-eighth time in a row. When the hour was up I rose to unpack my violin. I played for a long while, another failed imitation of a hill song, or perhaps a mountain song, but once I had failed it a dozen times over something suddenly changed in my routine.

I halted in my task, for the first time in an uncounted and uncountable number of days, and looked at my sister's corner of the room.

She was not painting, but had been. What she did in that particular moment was nothing. Her hands had fallen to her lap, brush threatening to fall from her limp grip, and she stared at what she had just made. I looked at it for myself and saw one of the things from my dreams, a stunted pale monster with a mouth that stretched from one ear to the other to bare rows of jagged teeth. It was in much greater clarity of course, but I was sure that it was the same being. It was hairless, its ears were but holes on each side of its head, and its eyes were grey as the stone. It looked out from a backdrop of blackness and I shivered as I looked at it.

Her eyes turned towards our mother, who sat silently before her own painting. The subject was identical, another one of the pale creatures, but the minute eccentricities in their styles separated the two. Our mother turned to look at her. Her eyes flitted from the painting to my sister's face and back again, perhaps as many as a dozen times as I watched. My sister took in a long, shaky breath and let it out slowly, loudly.

Our mother leapt up suddenly, ripped away the piece of canvas, and shredded it to pieces in her hands. She wailed, wordless. A single empty shriek had suddenly obliterated so many weeks, months, and years of silent work. When the painting was in a thousand pieces, she staggered to the middle of the room and ripped at her hair while we three watched. Tufts of black hair came free and fell to the ground around her. Words formed from her shrieks now, "No more! No more! No more! Never again! Never again! Never again!" She spun on my sister and pushed her aside to pull at her painting, tearing the canvas straight down the middle to leave half of the pale thing snarling at me. The half she had ripped away was nothing but tatters within moments. "Destroy it! Destroy it all!" she screamed and approached me where I sat, violin still gripped in taut, bloodless fingers. My heart lurched as I realized that she meant to break it. In that moment I knew that I would do quite anything to protect my beloved tool, this thing that represented my single purpose in absolute, this thing that had become an extension of my own being.

From overhead came the overwhelming sound of stone scraping against stone. I was able to halfway look up in that single moment of distraction to see that a deep darkness yawned above, and with it, cold wind kissed my face.

My mother keened, and I looked back to her. Something vast and grey . . . nay, not grey like the stone but shining silver . . . descended from the blackness into her, driving through her body to smash into the floor. The stone shattered beneath the force of it, and it pierced deep, setting the stone to thrumming beneath me. I looked at the silver thing and saw that it was all metal, and so thick around that as it pierced my mother's body it had nearly split her in two. Her feet remained on the ground, but her body had been bent all the way backwards by the force of the needle. She hung there, spasming, but she was quite dead, and those spasms were the last twitches of death taking her. The needle slowly, even gently, recoiled then, lifting my mother up with it to leave only a spatter of gore across the room and a deep hole wider around than my forearm in the floor. I looked up as she disappeared into the gaping blackness and beheld that great eye from my dreams, that thing which I hold chiefly to blame for transforming those dreams into terrors. It looked down on us for a few long moments and in that look was . . . irritation. It was gone in the next instant, and the stone ceiling passed overhead to settle back into place.

The next day, I returned to my task. I choose a different record, an elegant symphony. The blood is gone and the hole in the stone has been repaired, but not by us. When my listening hour is up I move to take out my violin and notice that my sister has not been painting. She is only looking at a piece of canvas marred with a few half-hearted gashes of color. She rises and turns to look at me, then my brother. She seems perplexed by something. I begin to ask what she is doing, but before I can get the words out, she breaks the brush in two and thrusts both jagged tips into her throat. She bleeds out in minutes. We make no attempt to save her for we know that we cannot. The effort is beyond us; there would be no point.

I often wonder which of we two remaining siblings will go next. Will it be with self-inflicted violence or will we be divinely punished for some mysterious, sudden outburst? Sometimes, I pause in my task and my bow hand shakes. I feel fragile in these moments, but other times, I notice my brother's extended pauses when pencil stops scratching against paper.

Perhaps it will be for the best if it is me. My nightly terrors have grown worse, and I see my mother and sister among the pale things. I only hope that there will be violins and records and fields of wheat wherever I go and no more of the infernal, unfeeling stone.

MIDWEST MACABRE

Like a plume of putrid black smoke rising over a distant horizon, dread rises in me. It coils in my stomach, a serpent of disquiet wound on a bed of acid, climbing up through the tubes and passageways of my body to nest just beneath my brain. Most days, I don't pay it any mind; I can almost pretend it's not there. But there always comes a day when it reminds me where it lives.

The population sign in my hometown says there are six hundred and thirty-two people there, but it has said that for at least twenty years now. A few feet past the sign is an enormous tree, ripped up at the roots to lean most of the way across the ditch that runs to the side of the highway. Storms with enough fury to tear up trees that big used to be a rare thing. The kind of thing men talked about in the mingling minutes before they went to work. In the gas stations, the coffee shops, the garages. We all wonder what's causing the change. Some of us know. The summers are hotter, the winters are colder, and the storms rage more fiercely; we all know it's different. If I wanted children, I might wonder at the horrors they'll see in the terrible future. Perhaps I'll see only a glimpse of it, if I'm lucky. Maybe I'm seeing it now, maybe these are the glimpses I wish away from my mind for comfort. Instead, I think of other people's children and grandchildren. Empathy is cruel. Selfishness is easy.

Every morning, I look out my window at rolling fields and sunlight gleaming off the blades of dark green grass and think all is well. And then I drive to work, into the world, and all seems so completely, utterly, absorbingly unwell. It's wrong, all wrong.

W
R
O
N
G

People here go to work, then they work, then they work some more, and then they go home and drink and watch their marriages fall apart in a place that seems to get smaller every year instead of bigger. The old are the ones who linger. They bought in during better times when houses were something most folk could reasonably expect to afford. Not in houses with white picket fences, that era was long past even before their time, but houses with green yards and grandchildren to play in them and other old friends to drink coffee with every morning at whatever local meetup is still in business. The young leave or give up. Every few years, someone works up the courage to open a restaurant or a grocery store, and it inevitably dies by the next summer. The farmers are running out of local labor. The help has fled to the cities where the wages are better, so they turn to fancy programs that bring in white Christian men from South Africa and Ukraine, men who are promised they'll get to bring their family over in a matter of years if all goes well. It may come true.

I drive down roads that run straight as an arrow for miles, and strewn all along it are desecrated trailers and aging houses, yards peppered with emptied beer cans and discarded children's toys. The pickup trucks and used cars often have bright red Republican political stickers. Always men who would never shake their hand without washing it after. One dump sports a flagpole from which flies the American libertarian's standard, the coiled snake on yellow with the tagline "Don't Tread On Me". Every square foot of unhoused soil in this area is farmland and the one beacon of wealth is that pure white two-story home that sits beside a splay of grain bins and parked farm equipment. It's perfect, so perfect and white, but the rust shows on the bin's roof at a football field's length away. It is the manor of a feudal ruler in my mind, a land baron, a warlord. That perfect white paint becomes hideous in that light. It was painted and maintained by men who will never live in a home that looks like it.

The most beautiful thing a person can see though, is when you're parked at a railroad crossing, waiting for the endless stream of metal to pass. The art on the sides of the cars passes you by like a gallery, and you get a sampling of it all. Some people, the ones parked in the line ahead and behind me perhaps, see graffiti as a degenerate art. It defaces a symbol of industry, unasked for, unwanted. I see the big, bold lettering and colors as messages from another world. Yes, even "James Parks Dick in Ass". They don't know me and I don't know them, but we both know the other is out there. It's "out there" or "in there", one or the other. It's like they're sending me letters, or a cipher perhaps. A friendly cipher in this case, not like those ones the Zodiac Killer sent. But I don't know how to read them, and I've never tried to send something back.

There's a ten-mile stretch of highway between two towns near me where it feels like every other house is burned out, collapsed, or just abandoned. There's one on the closer end to me, where a homeless man has built a makeshift shelter from the remains of a dilapidated home. Two big pieces of wall are leaned against each other, triangular, and two smaller pieces in the spaces between to make this strange little spired hut, skinny but twice again the height of most men. Chunks of broken fence have been stood up around it. One of the small walls still has a window. A fireplace is constructed outside, and it always seems to be smoldering. It is as much an expression of the American dream as a perversion of it. One begins to wonder if the dream, as we once knew it, was just the mask it wore, a false face. We let the mask rot so long that it fell away entire, and behold, now, a dream's waking.

The man himself is how most people imagine the homeless; bearded and unclean. They imagine, too, unclean thoughts in his head, his intent to kidnap and rape their daughters, to break into their homes to steal their silver and gold and crisp green dollar bills, to spontaneously murder someone outside a gas station, to smother their widowed, isolated grandfather in his sleep after breaking in because they know he doesn't hear well and won't hear the intrusion. I imagine instead a dejected hermit or a shaman mixing herbs by firelight. He speaks to arcane spirits, to a god whose name is known to few. If I came to him by darkness, I think he would tell me my future, for five dollars.

The mundane has begun to hold a sinister energy for

me. I drive into the city, and at a stoplight there is a truck in the lane next to me with a trailer attached. On the trailer is a car identical to the one I sit in as I look at it, even down to the same layer of dirt on the lower sides. I swear to myself later that it even had the same guitar ornament hanging from the rearview mirror.

An ordinary day comes, deep in farm season. The crops are planted and begin to climb from the earth, more every day. It's an ordinary errand for me, too, to drive south into Arkansas and pick up some parts in some town I've never heard of. You can find a parts store every other mile where I come from, but this time, there's something special and it's far away. The highway shoots straight and true through a heartland of bean and rice fields for half a hundred miles. There's not one town on that road before my destination, but for just about every one of those miles I can see a smoke cloud, coal black, climbing above the distant horizon. That devil in my gut seems to sense it and climbs up, tenderly, towards my brain. My stomach tightens when I feel it shifting. All I can see is that cloud, and I know it's coming from exactly where I'm going. I don't know what went wrong, but something did. I don't believe there's a man in the country that can look at a cloud like that and think it's normal.

On the way back, doing a hard seventy up the blacktop, I see a car pulled over on the side of the road. A young man in blue jeans and a T-shirt runs towards something crawling across the blacktop away from him. I zoom by. It looks like a cat, but its back legs aren't working, and it's dragging itself along with just its front claws. It's orange and barely bigger than a kitten. A quarter mile on, I see another one doing the same thing, another cripple. I wonder if that young man is going to help both of them. I wonder if I would have helped them if I hadn't seen him helping already, but, truthfully, I know I wouldn't because I didn't even slow down at the first.

At the end of days, I preside over the land of the Unliving.

A King over the Working Dead.

An additional unhoused story . . .

UNDER A FUNERAL MOON
WITH MICAH S. VERNON

THE SEAFORT OF THE BIGHT SAT UP AGAINST A CLIFF taller than its towers, its walls climbing out of the rock shelves overlooking the bay, shores extending like pincers into the ocean. Tunnels and storerooms had been carved in the stone until no one living recalled just how far into the earth they went. The curtain wall facing the bay stood tall and solid as any mighty fortress of men and all who approached from that side presumed the nest impenetrable, but around the two gatehouses were great cloven wounds in the stone, so large that they could only have been made by the weapons of a giant, that left instead three entrances each to the north and south.

So it was that the men who would be its new administrators, marching with their own wounds and weariness in tow, in scuffed armor that still shone in sunlight, saw first its weaknesses and shared a collective groan knowing a great deal of work awaited them. Their commander surveyed the damage at a distance, his thoughts his own. *Such a little thing, for peace.*

————

WITHIN THE WALL, the buildings crouched low to the ground like tortoises as if bracing for some seeking impact. The storerooms and armory were windowless and one had to descend a short stair to the floor from the outside grounds, as it burrowed slightly down to couch their structures. The ceilings of these rooms and the keep's central hall seemed lower than they should be and the men walked them stooping reflexively, feeling an instinctive pressure on their necks and shoulders. The fireplace lay cold and dry, and rats ran the boundaries of every room. Many of the men were tall northlings and they instantly detested the conditions which seemed to grip tight around them, that shrunk them, that said they were not welcome.

Three towers stood in command of the design, all of them stabbing up along the western wall against the pale cliffside. The Commander's home would be in the Tower of Eyes, named so for the pairs of slit windows up its seaward face that studied the surrounding land. He would have given much for a balcony where he could sit and watch and feel the ocean air on his skin, but instead he had been given a stuffy, suspicious spy-place to govern from. It would have suited an inquisitor better than an officer looking forward to a little quiet.

Whereas the shorter towers maintained a healthy distance from the rock face, the cliff seemed to grow around the Tower of Eyes, clutching at it as tenaciously as a lover. Gulls nested in its siblings, but shunned its own peak. Dust seemed to slough from its bricks and mortar, but soaked into the stone everywhere else. The sun's rays rarely found it, never truly warmed the face peering out from its shadowed recess.

The Commander climbed the spiral staircase to his

solar, a dreadfully long thing, circling forever and ever, but paused before the door. It was fragile, made of old wood almost ready to collapse in on itself, the hinges rusted down to the most brittle of metal. He thought to remind himself to have it replaced. Though something else held him there and a thought came unbidden. *I shouldn't be here. I should be home.* Another thought answered it, its tone different. *What is it that awaits you there? Nothing.* A third voice echoed in the halls of his mind. He was not sure whose. *The one who needs you most.*

The pattering of boots against the stone steps brought him back. "Is it locked, lord?"

He tried the door and let it creak slowly inward. The room rested still and dim and silent beyond. Cobwebs wrapped around the door frame but elsewise he was surprised at how clean the place was relative to the ancient coating of dust that covered everything else in the keep. Only the frailest light beamed through the eye windows and converged on the desk, where a heavy tome lay neatly straightened and waiting. Shelves packed with hundreds of texts covered the walls, more books than he could likely read in a lifetime.

"Are you an avid reader, lord?"

He went in and paced along the shelves, a finger wiping along an edge at waist height and coming up only a little grimed. He cleansed it on his leg. "It was not my habit, no. Though I suppose I will have time enough to start."

The soldier stepped in behind him, flint eyes scanning the room. He stood straight-backed and unbreakable. "I'll have a mattress brought up for you immediately, lord."

He glanced at the empty wooden frame, the wood along one flank snapped inward. "Time enough for that. Get the lads settled in first. We're in no hurry here. The war is won." He went to the window and looked out at the rippling waves of the bay. The roofs of huts peeked over the rocks to the north. "The locals are a fishing folk I imagine."

"Yes, lord, I should think so."

"But not the bay?"

"Lord?"

"They have nothing built along the shores that I can see, nor do I spy any fishermen. There's enough to catch inside, I can see them jumping from here." He paused, thoughtful. "We might as well set some men to the task. Any man with the desire is free to on his own time, but assign a dozen men that daily duty as well. We may grow sick of seafood, but we will not starve." Dark, featureless figures peeked out of the rocks near the village and held vigil a while. *My smallfolk*, he thought. The Commander watched them, thinking that somehow their eyes sought him out specifically and not the regiment scattered about the fortress below. *They would know me. And I shall know them, in time.*

———

OLD SER ORIC bled onto the stone upon the shore. His blood had darkened with age, blueblack in the light of the crescent moon. Dripping from his naked wrist, he wrapped the wound and fingered a sigil into the blood, muttering invocations under his breath—the names of gods all but forgotten, words only known in the whispers of his worship. Many years past, this shore would have been lined with faithful men of the Bight, bleeding upon the stones. But now he kneeled alone. He looked to the lights of the fisherfolk on their distant shelf and wondered if they, too, had abandoned the old faith.

He breathed sharply and made the sign of the new moon across his face—to signify the sickle, or the scythe—and sheathed his sword. Still sharp, still faithful.

After all these years.

"As we reap, so must we be reapt."

Ser Oric stood, knees popping with exertion. He made his way to the battlement, the stairs mocking each labored step. When he finally reached the top of the wall, walking into position, leaning on the crenellations, he settled down.

Sitting upright in his armour against the parapet, he addressed Melwyn, a soldier three decades his junior, "Wake me when it's my watch."

"Ye need no' sleep he—"

"Wake me," he said, "when it's my watch."

His leathers still chafed. Gorget and pauldron pinched his neck when he tried to rest his head.

After all these years.

———

He woke to the sound of waves crashing.

"Help me up," he said.

"It's no' yer watch yet, auld man."

"I said help me up, you faithless dog."

"A'reit, a'reit, keep yer pants oan." Melwyn bent to hoist him up from his underarms, and Ser Oric struggled to stand on sleeping legs, leaning once more on the crenellations to steady himself.

"My father served here, you know," Ser Oric said, steady now, looking out at the threshing, winedark sea. "Once upon a time."

"Did 'e now?"

"He did. And I see you have a habit of questioning your elders, lad."

"Aye, an' ah see they hev a habit o' sendin' deid men t'this barren shore tae defend a pile o' rubble. First yer father an' now you."

"It used to be an honor to serve here in the Bight," he said. "Men would bring their wives, daughters. Girls would give their first blood on the shore; newborns were baptized by the sea." He paused a long while, breathing in the salt air. "Yes, a knight could be proud to be assigned here, once. It was a sign of prestige. A sign of trust."

"Aye? An' whit must it be now, then, eh? a curse?"

Ser Oric didn't respond. He kept looking out at the sea, and breathed deeply of its salt. Above, the moon watched them through parted clouds.

"Ah wonder whit it says aboot masel'," Melwyn continued, "knowin' they sent me here wi' the likes o' you."

———

A squat, wide-stanced man stood on the shoulder of the road they had marched in on the previous morning. He watched from nearly out of eyesight of the north gate as their party approached, three ahorse and a dozen footmen behind with polearms against their shoulders and short swords at their hips. The sun was already low in the sky, the shadows from the cliff and towers reaching eagerly towards the bay. Riding, the Commander watched the little man who seemed not so little, somehow. In his loose-fitting shirt tied at the hip with a stretch of rope resting lightly atop his hips he seemed bulky and wide and solidly entrenched wherever he might choose to stand. A wiry, heavy beard touched the center of his chest. The Commander pictured a torso furred like a bear, belly like a keg. There was something of a dwarf in him, though he was still north of five feet by some small figure.

The Commander had doffed his armor at last after a long year of campaigning and now felt freed in raiment he would wear at home, though the make was not accorded with the wet warmth here. His aide was likewise garbed more casually, but seemed even more frustrated with the endless sweat. The younger man was well disciplined and sat straight in the saddle, but his fingers played irritably with the saddle horn. The aide caught his gaze and let his fingers fall still against his thigh. On his other flank, the Commander heard his captain grunt gutturally at something.

The squat man was to guide them to the village. When they stopped in conversational distance, the man explained that the path was little more than a mule trail through the treacherous rock shelves that jutted up like teeth as far as they saw. It was wide enough for their horses, but they would need to go single file. The captain urged his mount first after their guide. He had not felt secure enough to go unarmored yet, but even had he worn only a shift of wool the Commander knew he would take any blow before him gladly. They eyed the rise to their north where it would have been an easy thing for a handful of archers to shoot them down, their minds still warm in the sheath of war. He wondered how long it would take for them to adapt to peacetime again. Every return seemed like it took longer, and the yearning for the routine simplicity of a campaign gnawed.

They came out below a small cliff and found the village to be a long arrangement that snaked along the coast for half a league, the houses spaced wide apart and many docks and huts close to the water. Their guide lay back in the shade of a large rock and watched them ride down through the village. The footmen tightened back into formation and the aide moved up to within three hand-spans of his horse's nose. They slowed their pace for the Commander to take in the place. A few boats lingered out at sea, desperate. Wary-eyed folk watched them pass as they gutted and scaled their catch for the day, their glistening hands working methodically even as their gaze trailed the newcomers. One woman worked at a shockingly large fish with elaborate pale blue spines longer than her knife. The Commander paused to watch her. "A fine haul. Your husband must be a skilled fisherman."

She looked at him dully, her hands never stopping. "My man's long dead. Boys too. This was mine."

Taken aback, he only nodded and rode on.

They came on a stout fellow with a longsword belted at his waist further on. The buckle was rusted steel inlaid with silver and it struck him as stranger even than the presence of the sword itself. His captain began to call out to the man, but he disappeared down an alley and when next they saw him he had made his way far down the beach. The aide asked him if he wished the man pursued and questioned, but the Commander dismissed the notion. *A soldier's sharp questioning. Ah, that's the last thing this day needs.*

They came to a smithy that sat the crest of a hill bisecting the village and they looked down the remaining stretch that strung along between houses and huts identically to that which they had just passed through. The smith, a bald-headed, bald-faced man with one arm half again as muscled as the other, hammered at a horseshoe, heedless of them. The captain dismounted and approached.

"Smith! Know you where we may find the village spokesman?"

The smith stopped and looked at him, then at them. The Commander saw his eyes pick over the weapons they carried interestedly. "Who'd that be?" he said, looking back at the Captain.

The Commander spoke, "I was told a man named Harmond would speak on your behalf."

"Ah. He's not here."

"Now was the appointed time. Where might he be?"

The smith stretched his neck distractedly, returning to his work. "North, like as not. The tradesman road to market. What we do not eat, he takes."

The Commander sighed. The sun was touching the horizon. He did not relish a return through full dark. "Let us away. I will speak with this man on another occasion."

The Captain lingered a moment. He drew off his helm and held it in the crook of his arm to let the smith have a look at his face, framed with lank, sweaty hair. His bushy mustache hid his lips until he spoke. "I had not thought to find a swordsmith in a place such as this."

The smith spared him only a glance more. "And you still have not."

The Captain shifted the balance between his legs. "No? I saw a lad only moments ago who carried a blade, a longsword of well-make."

"T'were no make of mine."

The Commander slumped back in the saddle and watched figures mill across the street downwind of them or drift in from the beach. Few spared them more than a glance. A breeze swept in and kissed his neck and he almost felt cool again.

———

THE COMMANDER's eyelids wavered in the candlelight, no longer dancing from left to right over the weathered pages before him. The writing was dry enough, but it was not the content that made him drowsy, merely the late hour. Before dinner, with what remained of dusk's light, he had parsed the shelves for attractive reading. Whomever had stocked them, likely several whomever's given their quantity, seemed to have been drawn to folk-lore, but he had little appetite for the superstitions of the smallfolk. There was such a thing as rural wisdom, but one had to dig deeply for it. Inevitably, it seemed, he was drawn back to the heavy work that had greeted him from the desk top. It conveniently concerned the patch of land he now governed, a history of both the construction of the fortress and settlement of the Bight, of the culture that he would soon court among the locality. He set to the task of reading it, thinking it only right to know as much as he possibly could of that which he now held sway over.

Once, he might have found himself effortlessly awake long into the hours of dark, a byproduct of many years of night watch duty. Now . . . he felt the weariness of age creeping after him.

He closed the book and went to the window, habitually thinking of the watchmen on duty below. He hoped to find none of them dozing at their post already. The last thing he wished was to have to administer discipline only days into his occupation. To stay that thought, he instead looked out over the water that had stilled by night, and at the low crescent moon beyond. Its light cast long down from the horizon and caught in the space between the two land pincers that threatened to clamp shut access to the sea. From there the sliver expanded until the middle of the bay where it closed steadily back together all the way to the beach. The effect was of an enormous cat-like eye looking up from the bay into the stars.

He stared, transfixed, until a head, silhouetted black

against the moonlight, dipped above the surface of the water at the apex of the eye.

A moment later, it was gone. Not even the water rippled where it had been.

He blinked, thinking it a figment of his tired mind and eyes. But on the shore to the northeast were distant torch flames; one, two, three, four he counted before they dipped and blinked out.

He retired to bed with a throbbing temple and troubled thoughts.

———

HE LIFTED his head to regard the little man. "Pardon, you say they call you what?"

"Harmond Fewfingers," the man said, flashing a hand over his chest crowned with only three of them; his thumb, ring finger, and pinkie. "Needlemaws are well-named."

The Commander scratched an eyebrow. "A fish was it?"

"Aye, a devilish bugger. Elsewhere the fish bid nary a farewell to their kin when the nets and poles draw them up, but somes here take issue with the lowly fisherman."

How lowly can a fisherman be in a place where fishing is the only trade? He left the thought there. Harmond had a friendly manner, but he distrusted a man so quick to smiles. Perhaps he was simply used to the black humors of soldiers. *He does not call me lord either.* His eyes fell back to his letters. The words blurred. It was a small impossibility that his noble betters all seemed able to include advice, requests, demands, condescension, and false concern all into single letters. He preferred the tiresome history book. *I'm just a soldier.*

Harmond had crossed to the slit window and peered

down. "You ought not waste your men's time with fishing. Buy from us! We take in so many fish of a season we know not what to do with them all. This old place needs to be set in working order first."

Nay, no fisherman, but a fishmonger. Best not to make any enemies so quickly though. He spoke gently. "I'm happy to buy or trade with you, but it would be more . . . financially sound for us to fill our own tables to an extent. We have no shortage of men and in peacetime I find it most prudent to keep them occupied. Men were made to build, I've heard."

There was a small silence when he finished speaking so he looked up at Harmond again. The man was watching him, expression flat, then seemed to snap from it a moment late. A brilliant smile bloomed across his face. "Here," he said, gesturing out the window. "We were made to fish. I wish you luck, my friend. May our dealings be long and fruitful. It has been quite some time since last we had a castellan here." And with that, he swept from the room. The word "lord" had still never slipped from between his lips.

———

SUMMER RAINS and Old Ser Oric spat imprecations on the stone. He chanted his bitter psalm ad infinitum, *as we reap, as we reap,* while the storm churned and sloshed the terrible sea behind him. Holding his blade against his palm, he stood and turned to the shore.

Backlit briefly by a flash of lightning, a figure stood within the shifting waters.

Ser Oric slid his sword long against his open hand and dropped it to the sand as he walked towards the tumultuous tide.

———

"Ye're late fur yer watch, auld man."

"On time, you mean to say."

"Aye. Fur the first time."

Ser Oric grunted.

The younger man spat.

"Thought ah saw summat down by the shore."

"My nightly prayer."

"Aye. So thir's two o' ye now?"

———

A GASP of thunder brought the Commander up from the desk, the great ponderous tome his cushion. Spittle pooled in the little vale between the pages. The letters were a blur. Shapes danced at the edges of his vision. He wiped his mouth and rose, loosening the lacings of his doublet. He looked over the book again, bent to mark his page, and closed it. A sealed letter sat near the candle that hadn't been there when he was awake. He picked it up and looked at the image pressed into the blood red wax. A tremor crept into his hand and he threw it back onto the desk as if stung. *Gods, I thought . . . I thought I had more time.* His breathing grew harsh and he turned away, blinking fast.

A heavy rain raged against the fortress and flashes of lightning lit the room. He staggered to the window drunkenly and looked out, needles prickling his face through the narrow aperture. The waters of the bay raged and threw waves against the rocks again and again as if furious they could not reach the fortress perched above. A man paced the southern walkway, sending torch-light shadows dancing across the stone. Every watch was three men, a cautious number relative to their post. The seaside wall and northern corner were still and silent and black. He cursed and began to turn away, meaning to send his door guard down to wake the watch officer when a shadow shifted in the alley between the barracks and the storeroom. Something hobbled free of the little pocket of deep darkness, treading close to the shadows away from the moonlit yard but, too late, brushed by the low glow from the barrack's windows for a moment. To be a man, he thought it must be a very large one wrapped in a heavy fur cloak, or several. And for a cloak to gleam strangely in that pygmy light . . . but he felt the warm ocean air lick his face through the window, it was always so warm by the sea.

"Alarm!" he cried through the window. "Intruder in the yard!" He saw the torch-walker to the south turn at the sound of his voice and the shadowed figure stopped in its tracks, still obscured. The Commander ran to the door, ripped it open, and ordered his guard down to the courtyard to wake the officers. When he returned to the window, he found the yard empty but for the lone watchman scanning it with his flame. A second figure dashed across and flung the barracks door wide.

Within the hour, he had half a dozen of his officers crowded into his solar. "Who had the assignment tonight?" he demanded.

"Young Nevill you saw yourself, lord. The lad is shaken, but sound. Elsewise it was Ser Oric and Melwyn."

He heard cries from outside and went to the window. A figure was limping over the seaside wall repairs as men rushed to meet them. He recognized Ser Oric a moment later, that queer knight-mystic. *There's one. Now where's the other?*

Ser Oric had found Melwyn tucked in a little cave among the rock shelves closest the beach, perhaps washed off the shore by the roiling sea. Every one of his limbs had been broken, his skull stove in, and his chest sundered open through plate, mail, and leather alike. Half his insides were mutilated and the other half missing entirely. The Commander ordered a small burial service and insisted that the night watch be doubled to six men from then on.

———

THE MEN HAULED STONES. Some in foul weathers; some with strained humor. Melwyn's death had soured the morning, and in the wake of the evening's storm, they danced around puddles thick with mud as the sun scorched the stones. As such, the refortification was slow work. These men were not masons—they were soldiers, and as such, comported themselves with the dignity of soldiers. A group gathered round, leveling punches at one such digni-fied: Johann of Northern Star. Short of stature, and not exceptionally broad, he stood unwavering as his fellow men tried, one by one, to cast him down. Blow by blow to his thick skull left him nought but a smile full of blood.

"I thought you lot were soldiers, not little boys," he laughed.

Young Gelding stood before him next and broke his hand against Johann's jaw. He screamed.

"Mayhaps we should fortify the wall with him," Flat-foot said as the men gave up with a groan and went back to their labor.

"About time you lousy pricks came t'help us," the Captain said. A few men grumbled agreement, but their hearts weren't in it. Young Gelding approached, nursing his broken hand, and asked leave, but the Captain denied him—"If you're stupid enough to break your hand against our Northern Star, you can bloody well kick the stones to the wall"—but after a few minutes of whimpering, the

Captain relented and let him seek treatment. "But your hand's not so pained you can't find other work. Might be they'll let you help in the kitchens. Just try not to piss in Johann's stew."

"He'd need to find his cock first," Johann said.

The men laughed as Young Gelding retreated, then talked amongst themselves.

"What are we do if we come under attack?" one asked.

"Build faster", said Flatfoot.

———

WHEN THE SUN had reached its zenith overhead, Ser Oric, ever-clad in his armour, approached the men at work.

"The tin man!" Johann jibed. "This here's work for those of able flesh. You should seek shelter before the sun boils you alive in your plate."

"You cast aspersions on a knight of the Order of the Virgin Moon?" Ser Oric said.

Johann spat at Ser Oric's feet. "A knight in name only. No better than a common soldier—nay, less, even."

Ser Oric's hand fell to his sword hilt. "I warn you not to test me, young man."

"Have at it then, *old* man."

"Enough of this," the Captain said. "Johann, you'd learn well to not disrespect your superiors."

"Why's he even here, Captain? What need have we for this mummer knight? Performing queer rituals by the shore every evening—it's unnatural. I trust him not, Captain, and neither should you."

"Ser Oric's motivations for being here are none of your concern, Johann. You should feel honored to have such a prestigious knight among our ranks."

"A cursed agent of the church, I say. Here to spy and

sow dissent. And what of Melwyn? By all accounts, *Ser* Oric here was the last to see him alive."

"One more word out of you, Johann, and I'll have you rebuilding the wall by yourself. I'll brook no argument. Understood?"

Johann stood silent.

"Good," said the Captain. "Ser Oric—what can I do for you?"

"Your boy," Ser Oric said, "with the broken hand."

"Young Gelding, Ser, what about him?"

"Regrettably, we are down a man on the wall, and I cannot abide a soldier without a posting. I should like him to take on watch duty tonight."

"As you say, Ser Oric."

The men watched Ser Oric as he walked slowly back to the keep; to depths unknown.

When he was gone, Johann dared speak. "Captain, you don't believe all that horseshit about feeling honored to have that old bastard among us, do you?"

"Not a word."

———

Days passed. Men had reported seeing Young Gelding with Ser Oric on the wall at night, but come morning he was always absent. No one had tended to his hand; no one had seen him in the mess. Ser Oric had been seen on occasion, passing the odd man by in the bowels of the fort, but for now he was nowhere to be seen. A few soldiers, in an unofficial search, scattered throughout the fort, and Flatfoot found himself lost in darkened corridors, deep, with only a lantern to light his way.

Where behind the fort lay infinity.

At the beginning, when he found a solemn door at the

back of the keep, it opened to a wide and bricklaid hall dotted with doorless rooms filled with spiders' webs and empty sacks, barrels, and crates. But as he went on, the halls carved deep into the rock of the Bight often diverged in multiple directions, splitting innumerably within themselves, each passage getting narrower and narrower. He had a path though, a trail: the unpaved floor was soft and damp so close to the sea. Footprints, freshly made, led him through the labyrinth.

He came to a passage with a steady decline into deep waters. The lantern held high before him, he saw no end in sight. He threw a small pebble into the pool and watched the water ripple and shiver further into the abyss.

"Well," he said, hoping his own voice might comfort him as it echoed over the water. "The lads'll not believe this one."

He dipped one of his moccasined feet into the water and felt his body prickle with gooseflesh—a result of the cold or the fear he knew not.

Trying not to swallow any of the saltwater, he waded through it as it deepened up to his neck. He could not swim, nor would he try to. He held the lantern above the surface, his heartbeat rising with each step as his feet sank deeper into the muddy silts of the cavern floor.

But even a measured step was not enough.

His weak foot buckled on a loose stone and his head went under and the lantern went with him. He panicked, thrashed, and sputtered as he struggled to bring himself back above the surface.

The light was gone. All was cold, immeasurable darkness. And he felt his lungs fill with water, searing icicles gripping his heart as consciousness left him.

———

He awoke spewing seawater, the sounds of the sea and an ocean breeze whistling its way through unfathomable caverns. And he heard another sound—a wet slavering; a baby's shallow cry, a covert moan. After a time, he struggled to his feet and followed the sound, guiding himself along the stony passage.

He saw a soft light ahead, and the passage opened up into a small grotto. As he entered he tripped on an unseen obstacle and fell to his knees and into puddles on the cave floor. When Flatfoot looked up he saw Ser Oric sat upon a weathered stool in the small light of a winnowing lantern. His cuirass on the floor, Oric moaned softly in agony, or rapture. Something suckled at his breast.

Ser Oric looked into Flatfoot's horrified gaze.

The something at his breast pulled itself away.

Ser Oric's right breast was raw with blood.

The creature looked at Flatfoot with a bloodred maw.

Flatfoot heard a sound indefinable behind him and stood, daring to look back at what had tripped him. There lay the corpse of Young Gelding, face torn to shreds, broken hand, untended, swollen and bruised upon his chest. The boy's belly was bloated and squirmed and rippled like water and sounded like the onslaught of the ocean.

As it burst, Flatfoot turned and fled towards the sounds of the tide and the something that suckled at Ser Oric's breast cried shrilly like a child.

———

Cloud cover left the beach dim, the moon peeking when it could through the veil. Torches walked the shoreline, a bobbing train of flicker-flames in the heavy wind. Halfway to the fort, they found the dead man.

They flipped him onto his back. The sand was black where his mouth had been. He had either lost the other parts of his armor or not worn them, for his mail shirt was the only metal on him. One among them stripped off the mail and held it bunched at his side, in spite of the rust. One other knelt at the corpse's side and grasped his face with three fingers, the two littlest and the thumb. Helpless nubs separated the two from the one. He turned the pale face to him, the corpse-eyes closed like in slumber. Gently, he pried open the mouth and looked in at the ruin.

"The little ones, they take the soft morsel inside," he explained to his companions, some of whom well knew. "They pry out the teeth that get in the way. This one has some yet."

"We should give him back," said the man who had taken the mail shirt.

"We will. Help me with him." The first man and three others each took a limb and began to tote him down the shoreline towards the fort. "Better this way. The soldiers won't be happy, but this will give them less reason to suspect us."

The fifth, who still held the mail shirt at his side like an unwanted sack, trailed behind. He looked out across the stillness of the bay and whispered to himself, "Nay. To the sea I meant. Give it back to them." He decided to give the shirt to his younger brother, who liked to play soldier.

———

IN THE DIM storeroom below the Tower of Eyes they laid Flatfoot's body across sacks of grain, for want of a table, and studied his injuries. The Commander stood in a corner away from the light, lips pursed, watching the sawbones work. The weight of his sword hung heavy at his hip again.

The sawbones stood straight and faced him. His eyes seemed beady, black little things and he paused seconds longer than most would before speaking. A studied unhurriedness. "Drowned, lord."

"Drowned?" he asked, rolling the word out slowly.

"Aye."

"Are men prone to losing their tongues and half their teeth in drownings?"

"No, lord, he did lose them, aye. I'm sayin' drowning's what done him in. His belly is full up with water. If it were just the mouth wounds he could have lived long enough to get back to us."

The Commander stared at him for a long while. "This man, who was posted inside the wall, who did not fish nor swim for fear of water, nonetheless was produced from the depths of the bay tonight, drowned? That is what you are telling me?"

The sawbones turned to the officers, who gawked absently with quivering fish mouths. "Were the lad truly afeared of water?"

One of them found his tongue. "I've heard it said before among the men. It was a frequent point of humor. It was a difficulty even to see him bathed."

"Well this is a blasted cursed place for a poor lad to be who's afeared of water."

"I fear no one thought to ask him first."

"Aye, might be someone should have."

The Commander turned and walked from the room, up the many steps of the Tower of Eyes to his solar, and slammed the door hard behind him.

———

HE READ all through the day. He should have known, there were too many pages dedicated to so inconsequential a place. And yet so little out in the open. Little preparation from the officer corps, not a peep from the Emperor's cadre of spies. The tome bore secrets, he could feel them approaching even as it was he who approached with each turned page. Somehow it was not him taking steps of any accord he could call his own, but it, this strange feeling, which compelled him on.

And then he found it.

A crescent moon.

The blood of women, naturally given.

Rituals of sacrifice. Peasant practices black enough for Hell's approval.

His aide knocked, entered, and spoke for several minutes all without the Commander realizing. He read on, oblivious, until the aide touched him on the shoulder. He flinched, eyes blazing at the man. "What is it?"

"Lord, Ser Oric is still missing."

"Still? How long?"

"All night and day, lord."

He pressed the heels of his hands into his eyes. "I was not told. Why was I not told?"

"Lord, you were. It was late discovered after Flatfoot, but I told you myself when we realized. You were . . . absorbed with your reading."

He went to the window, cursing himself. The eastern horizon was already black while some tints of orange were barely visible above his tower. *How long have I been at this foul business?* "You've searched the shores and the cliffs? What about the village? Mayhaps he stole away on some mischief there."

"I already dispatched men along the shore and cliff

tops and to the village. There was no trace and the fisher-folk did not seem to even know him."

A thought sprang suddenly from him like a leak. "The storerooms. They carve deep below, he may have fallen foul of a cave-in. Take as many men as you need and see it done." They both turned from each other, but the Commander spoke. "And Ser." The aide, no knight but who perhaps wished to be someday, looked back. "No man should be without his sword and armor this night. Even you." He looked to the wall where he had hung his own suit, collecting dust. *Even me.*

When the aide was gone, he instead went to the book again and, standing there with some small comforting distance between him and it, turned the page again and found a folded bit of yellowed parchment there in the crack between. He watched it, tucked there, and contemplated ignoring it entirely. Just closing the book on the whole matter and facing whatever may come with sword in hand. But in the end he drew it out and unraveled it in the candlelight.

Its visage deceives. Trust not in the moon's light and that which it illuminates, for shadows follow.

He donned his armor, taking too long with the fastenings. He was not so out of practice. Something was ill upon his ears, it keened distantly. He thought it had a tune for one insane moment. *Your imagination.* When he was done with the armor he slumped heavily in his chair, breathing strained. His eyes fell on the letter laid askew at the corner of the desk and something told him there was a moment that was passing, irrevocable. He reached out to it and paused, swallowed. Seeing the steel on his arm gave him courage. He felt a soldier again and took up the letter and broke the seal, pulled the candle closer.

My Lord Father,

I have been told that is how I must address you now, as a lord. I wanted to simply write "Father", but then I thought how furious Mother would be. Well, my Lord Father, I should first congratulate you on the fief you've been rewarded with. All those years away in service had to be rewarded somehow. I know that now, though I didn't expect it when I was younger. I have outgrown my foolishness you'll be happy to know. I thought you would just come home when your war was won or if it was lost I would never see you again. I suppose that's what I'm writing you about. For you to come home.

Mother is dead. I buried her. Me. I know this is not news to you. I am old enough to know that I am too young to have buried a parent. I expected it to be you we would bury, carved by the sword of some distant barbarian. You've been given a new duty instead. Well, you have a sacred one to your family first. Come home. I fear this will be to no avail and that I have not outgrown my foolishness after all, but know that I have tried.

Your son, Thomas

He was still from the tips of his fingers to his teeth when he finished reading, so he read it again and by the end he was trembling in every place instead. He wept and wiped the tears angrily away with the rough leather of his glove. When he tried to read it a third time he found his vision too blurry and tossed the letter in the floor.

He held his head in his hands and wept softly. The keening in his ears rose subtly until he realized it was a foreign noise and not some infernal piping in his skull, a harbinger of his damnation. The distant sound found a melodic shape, pitched high. His mind began to fog and fade and he laid his head down to rest.

———

IT APPEARED TO BREATHE. A death rattle. A labored

wheezing as a cold draught coursed through the splintered wood.

The men all looked to Johann as the Captain approached the door.

"Ser Oric?" the Captain called.

A cough. Sputtering.

He opened the door.

Blood quivered over Ser Oric's loosely fitted cuirass, hanging from him like iron flesh. The old man staggered out from caverns unseen, blooddrunk or dying, longsword in hand.

The Captain moved to carry the old knight but hesitated.

"Captain—" Johann warned.

In the darkness behind Ser Oric shadows moved like dust in a shaft of light. And a baby cried.

Ser Oric struck, sword swift in his aged hands, catching the Captain in his throat. Words that none could hear bubbled through blood on his lips as he collapsed, and Johann had nought but processed the situation before he felt Ser Oric's blade bite behind his knee. Johann lurched forward—Ser Oric behind him now—almost falling to the ground before catching himself and drawing his own blade and pivoting, just fast enough to catch Ser Oric's second blow. Pain shot through him; innumerable veins of agony.

He was far too aware of the darkness now at his back, but his mind couldn't linger on shadows as he held his ground against Ser Oric's onslaught—not through skill, but stubbornness. He could do little to maneuver each time Ser Oric lunged to pierce his butted mail, weakly sweeping aside the furious attacks as the old man grunted and coughed.

It was as Ser Oric lunged a final time that Johann finally heard the shadow-wrought screams of his fellow soldiers, smelt the iron of their gushing blood, felt the tip of the sword wading deep into the depths of his heart.

Johann's corpse had stood until the last of the soldiers fell. And when Ser Oric's sword withdrew, Johann of Northern Star, too, fell to unrelenting tides.

———

THE COMMANDER still splayed across his desk when he heard the heavy crash downstairs and distant screams flitting up the spiraling stair. He came to his feet in a rush, steel bared. Something thundered low in the tower again.

He went through the door and took the stairs slowly, the sword tip dancing ahead of him. At the bottom he found the door sundered from its hinges, lying against the lowest steps. His aide sprawled across it, blood gurgling through stilled lips and one arm ripped off at the shoulder. He still wore only his doublet. He cursed under his breath and drew a torch down from the wall and thrust it ahead of him into the dark of the entry room. A swath of blood painted the floor from one door to the other, the left leading to the storerooms and the right to the common room adjoining the tower. Muffled sounds issued from the latter. He went right.

The trestle tables had been knocked askew and bodies were strewn across the floor, all of them his men. The ruin of their bodies was difficult to look upon. Many, like his aide, had limbs torn away and others their throats ripped open. One man, even through a steel breastplate, had been separated diagonally across the chest. Another's helm had been squashed into his skull until the whole looked like a dripping red apple.

Across the room he caught movement and wet slurping sounds.

He crossed, torch and sword thrust ahead. Against the wall another of his soldiers slumped. His breastplate had been caved in and pulled apart and now a hunched form dug about in his insides. The Commander held when its shape came fully under the light, speechless. It was reptilian, bearing a thick, scaly hide marked with razored spines down its back and along its heavy draconian tail. Its eel-like neck extended into the dead man's chest cavity, where its head was entirely lost in the mess of torn steel and viscera. Its taloned hands rested on the man's hips like a lover's.

He gently laid the torch down beside them, eyes never leaving the feasting demon, but it didn't react. He held up his sword in a two-handed grip over his head and brought it hard down against its neck, chopping down to the bone. The demon recoiled from its meal, shrieking agony as its neck hung half-severed and spurting. It reeled back up to its full height, near twice again as tall as he, and he swung a fierce side long cut that drove deep from the other side, again striking the bone but this time severing through. Its freed, gore-drenched head flew across the room and the demon's body flailed wildly before toppling among the other corpses.

He walked out into the yard, where he found more of his men strewn across the ground and the ramparts, dead and fed upon, all. A blood trail led toward one of the breaches in the north wall. He followed through the breach and down over the rock shelves towards the moonlit beach, now crowded.

The demons were spread all along the length of the shore from one end to the other and they had brought dozens of the dead with them that they had thrust into the wet sand where the tide came in so that their lifesblood would drain back into the sea. Numbly, he walked down among them. They did not react to his presence, for their gaze was drawn fixedly out to the sea. A few torches peeked shyly among the rocks near the village. Near a low, flat rock, he found Ser Oric, leaning on his sword. He had stripped away his armor and the Commander could see a weeping red wound at his side. The Commander went down and knelt at his side and thrust his sword in the sand between them. They shared a look, two old soldiers in nicked armor, and then turned their eyes back to the water. To her.

In that same place he had seen a head appear those nights ago, now was a woman. He could see her from the waist up above the water, pale and nude and beautiful as the clearest night. An amber glow was in her eyes and through it he could see that those eyes were only for him, him forever, and he knew that he had always had them for there was the deepest familiarity there that he should have recognized in an instant. Even in the darkness he could see how golden and glorious and long her hair was, cascading over her shoulders and chest.

"Gods, she . . . her hair . . ." he said weakly, the words sloughing away from him even as he tried to speak their sounds.

"Black as a raven's wing. Black as the darkest night. Black as the deepest depths of the sea," said Ser Oric, smiling.

"No," he said, confused. "Gold. Her hair was gold. Is gold."

They looked at each other. A rumble came from beneath the earth and they turned back to see a series of ripples come across the surface of the water. The woman began to rise out of the depths then and where her waist should have attached to a pair of legs instead they beheld a squirming mass of leviathan tentacles in their dozens. She rose and rose ever higher until her form blacked out the moon's light. With her approach, a deep and terrible darkness reached out to embrace them.

————

WHEN NEXT MOONLIGHT fell across the bay, it found the waters still, the rocks peeking, silent, and the fortress, which had stood for centuries counted and uncounted, alone or in good company, empty.

And three chapters from "Through The Black Saloon".
A novel of horror on the American Frontier.

THROUGH THE BLACK
SALOON

PROLOGUE

THE RIDER URGED HIS HORSE ON AS HARD AS HE DARED, NO more than a trudge under the conditions of a hard down-pour slashing at his cheeks or any other exposed skin. They went nearly blind with only a thin sliver of moon peeking through the roiling clouds. His teeth ground against each other to stop from chattering and every few moments he would expel one of the many curses and condemnations he had tumbling around in his head. Still, he urged his mount on with one hand tightly gripping the flaps of his coat close around him.

He could feel May-Bell panting. She was tired, he knew. More than him, certainly, accounting for the distance they'd gone, but they couldn't stop even to breathe in this state. The rain was endless, an enduring assault on every one of their senses. He was glad for the time he'd been able to sleep in the saddle before the rain had really set in, tied in place for safety though he reckoned he could have managed without. He thought back to the rock crevice he had passed before nodding off that would have made for a fine campsite, but stubbornly he had insisted to himself on covering more ground before full dark. But then he had come on a miles-long stretch of plain with no cover in sight and the storm had crept up on him in his traveling slumber and now he was soaked down to the very marrow of his bones.

Truly, he should have stayed in that town up on the clifftop, but the thought of doing so made him shudder. In his short time among the townsfolk, he had seen all manner of queer behaviors, a pack of jittery mutterers who could barely manage a sentence in his direction. Some watched him with something less like suspicion and more like . . . longing. Others seemed not to even know he was there, nor anyone else. The only one with a semblance of normality had been the saloon owner, and his manner had been less than hospitable. Even the air up there seemed choked with a venom that coated the inside of his mouth and throat and made him want to scream.

A light appeared in the distance, tiny, dancing, a guiding star brought down to the earth. *Praise God,* he thought. "Praise God!" he screamed, the desperate sounds bursting from his throat with a madness and evaporating instantly in the gale.

Coffee. Hot, black, and steaming, that's how I want it. A warm bed, maybe a nice sit by a fire. Don't even need no supper tonight, I'll be just fine long as I'm dry and warm. The light was not all that far, that he felt relatively sure of, but he knew he had to be cautious driving May-Bell too hard in the darkness for fear of finding a ditch or an unlucky rock and breaking one of her legs. The thought of having to put her down in that terrible imagined scenario set the hairs on his neck to prickling. May-Bell had been his companion for many years and deep down he hoped they'd go out together, however the end came. But he didn't mean for it to be in this devil-made drenching and so he resigned himself to working his way through his respectable library of curses and counting the long minutes it took to finally near that distant spark.

But near it, he did. It proved to be a better shelter than he had dared to hope, a weathered but intact saloon with a single lit candle in the window, his guiding star. A stone well sprouted out from the earth a dozen feet from the structure. A bucket sat the sill of it and strangely did not shudder with the wind or threaten to fall in or without, but the rider hungered too much for shelter to linger on the thought. What a saloon was doing out there, something that should have been visible when he had first come on the plain in daylight, that he could not say, but he hitched May-Bell up where she would be shielded from the rain and was thankful doing it. A low structure sat beside the saloon, something he thought may have been a stable, but the doors were shut fast to him. Through the window he saw another candle burning on the bar and a shambling figure. He looked around, wondering if he had somehow found his way into a small town, but it was still impossible to make out the shapes of any other buildings with the rain beating down in sheets. He started to strip off his gun belt, thought twice, then belted it back on. *Don't know folks out here.* His spurs clinked as he approached the door and knocked the rain off his boots. He shook out his coat a little too and looked down at the spectacular puddle he would be leaving behind. The air that brushed his face as he pushed through the door was cool. A raw disappointment shot through him. *Shit. No fire.*

The door scraped shut and he immediately felt a familiar relief in that endless all-consuming downpour sound being muffled outside. In a blink, he was somewhere else. Another place, another age. His big brother waved their father's pistol over their heads, playing an outlaw or a soldier, he couldn't remember which. His mother looked through the kitchen window at them and he met her eyes as they split wide with panic. A bang and a burst of sparks, the sulfuric smell of gunpowder choking his nostrils. He was deaf for so long, his mother holding him with tears in her eyes, until he wasn't. He had thought it all part of the game.

The barman peered at him dully, an old bent-backed man with squinty little dark eyes that combed over the rider like he was taking the sum of a horse. "Howdy, mister," the rider said, forcing a stiff smile as he approached the bar. One of his boots tap-tapped lightly against the wood, a nervous habit. His teeth threatened to chatter. He clenched his jaw hard, willing away the crystal-lizing cold. *Goddammit, where's the fire? Just my luck to find the one sumbitch don't keep his house warm.* He looked around. There was light in a stairwell and sconced on the walls behind the bar. Three quarters of the room was bathed in deep shadow, but he suspected the mysteriously unlit fire-place existed thereabouts. If there was an inner balcony on the second floor, he could not see it.

"Good evening," the barman replied. His nails scratched at the countertop.

The rider chuckled awkwardly. The sound came out stilted, the bones in his face stiffened by disuse during the journey. "This evening ain't worth a damn, if you care for my opinion, but I'm glad to be out of the rain. Could I trouble you for something hot to drink? Coffee?"

The barman observed him, betraying little. "We have no coffee, but there's whiskey."

The rider's gaze drifted back down to the man's feverish scratching. *Is he writing something? Must not think overly of his establishment to be doing a thing like that.* Now that he was looking at it directly, the surface of the bar was nearly entirely webbed with marks that seemed to have some alien coherence to them the longer he looked. He lifted his gaze. Something was tickling in his gut and he was glad to feel the weight of the six-iron on his hip. A knife mirrored it on the other side, but he would prefer it not come to that, if it came to anything at all. He'd been in one knife fight in his life and would rather not make it two. "Whiskey will do," he allowed. The barman turned to the cabinet and regarded it carefully. He silently chose a bottle and then produced a shot glass from beneath the counter, filled the one with the other and pushed it his way. The rider drained it and watched as the barman filled another for him without comment. The rider drank that too and looked around. "Did I catch you fixin' to go to bed? What time is it?"

"No, sir. It is not so late."

He was trying to pick out the accent. It seemed European, but he had no particular ear for it past that guess. "I just figured because the fire was out. And I seem to be your only customer." His eyes drifted around the bar area, searching for a nameplate or something of that sort. "Where the hell am I anyway? Didn't see this place when I come out on the plain, before the rain kicked in. Come from Callum Point way, headed toward Mandred."

"It's just an old place," the barman replied. His eyes never seemed to stop watching the rider, though that one hand continued to scratch at the wood endlessly. Then his gaze broke suddenly, his eyes flickering for a moment to something over the rider's shoulder and then back again. "Excuse me a moment, sir. I will go retrieve some coffee for you."

The rider's brow furrowed. "Thought you said weren't no coffee?" but the barman had disappeared through a door beside the liquor cabinet before he could even finish the sentence. *Was he lyin' the first time or just misspoke?* Shrugging, he reached over the counter to retrieve the whiskey bottle, thinking to drink down one more gulp in the meantime.

"Sir, would you kindly put that back? Folk 'round here would consider it rude." a voice called from the darkness across the room, cool and sharp as the knife he wore. Goosebumps blossomed up his neck and he fought the urge to spin around. He managed a stiff turn towards the sound. A flame sprang to life from the dark, then drifted down a few inches to the wick of a candle. A man's face appeared in the newly born flame.

The rider slowly set both glass and bottle down on the counter. "Apologies," he said slowly.

The man looked at him down a long sharp nose. "I'll accept that on the part of our host." Though largely wreathed in shadow, most of what the rider could see of the man's face was unexceptional. There was a neat, dark beard and fair skin and he wore a black hat. But his eyes were different. From two hollowed out, shaded sockets stared eyes of amber. A wolf's color. The rider had never seen such eyes and so he assumed they were merely a light brown with the light playing some small tricks on his perception. "Take your hat off, sir. Let's look at you," the strange man said.

This man ain't my master, he thought, some anger welling up in his gut. He hesitated for several awkward seconds, then conceded on the grounds of not wishing to make any trouble. He tossed the hat on the counter and raised a hand to his scalp to make sure his hair wasn't sticking up anywhere. "You still got yours on," he said.

The man stared at him for a long while, not answering. Finally, he looked away, ruffling in his pocket for a few moments before presenting a cigarette. Slow and precise as a surgeon, he produced another match. He might have lit it from the candle burning before him, but he raked the nail of his thumb up its length hard and the tip struck alight on the first try and he lit the cigarette with it. Rather than lifting it to his lips though he placed it upright on the table, burning end pointed at the ceiling. It did not threaten to fall over. It did not even quiver.

The rider was unnerved but tried his very best not to show it. He was glad that his hands were tight in the pockets of his coat, as his fingers were a jittery mess. *Introduce yourself. Maybe that'll put things straight.* "Forgot my manners. My name is-"

"Quiet," the man commanded in a whisper that somehow cut across the room and stopped the rider in the midst of his sentence as surely as it would have if the man had roared at him. The man's yellow eyes fell to the cigarette and watched it burn its way down toward the tabletop. Seconds agonizingly ticked by in which the rider was too confused and nervous to do anything but stand there in silence. He drew his shooting hand out of his pocket and hung it there at his hip, but he dared not shift the flap aside and reach for his pistol.

When the cigarette was down to its last quarter, the man stood and plucked it up and took it deeper into the shadows. The light was no more than a tiny flare in the dark and the rider couldn't even see the fingers clutching the little brand. It dropped down a few feet and then went tumbling through the air to land somewhere that obscured it briefly. In the next instant, a flame roared to life over a stack of logs, illuminating a fireplace of stone. The strange man appeared in the light, kneeling and peering deep into the flames, ignoring all else. As he did so, the light was cast out in a gentle wave that revealed first two new figures, one to each side of the chimney, then four, then eight, and so on until the rider realized there had been more than twenty men settled in the shadows of the saloon. Their eyes were on him, every single one, and all were that same hungry, wolfish yellow.

Something flashed to his right, a loud accompanying crack, and the rider felt his knee erupt.

He collapsed, shrieking. "Goddamn you, you shit, you devil bastard, you sonofabitch, goddamn you," he heard coming out of his mouth but his mind was an inferno of agony. His eyes found their way to his knee for a moment and he saw the gory ruin that was left of it before averting them back to the ceiling. *Never gonna walk again. Never gonna ride again. Never gonna walk again. Never gonna ride again,* he thought again and again and again, struggling to find any other pattern of coherent thought but for those two terrible sentiments.

The man materialized above him, then several more faces beside him. He looked at the rider with something that might have been pity. In the others was only desire. Somehow, even in his state of near-madness brought on by the pain he knew it was a hunger he had never, and would never, know. A devious, terrible, and everlasting hunger.

"Why did you not shoot him in the head . . . or the heart perhaps? Make it clean?" the man asked, faint distaste in the question.

Someone answered, "The blood tastes sweeter when they suffer."

His face twisted slightly. "No, it doesn't," the man answered. "You just like it better that way." A pistol appeared in his hand and the rider stared up its barrel at the man who would kill him.

There was another flash and the sound of it was swallowed up by an even more terrible darkness, reaching out to hold him.

CHAPTER ONE

THE TRAIN TRACK SLICED ACROSS THE PRAIRIE FOR MILES, straight and sharp as an arrow. A northerly wind set the grass bending hard southward. Cole watched it bow like people in prayer from his perch on the rocky hillside that marked the western edge of the prairie and then let his gaze trace back to the track and follow its path until he saw the black serpent of shaped metal racing towards them. An endless stream of coal smoke issued from its skull, dark as a moonless night and thrice as evil. The train still liked a few minutes before it could pass them through the slim passage through the hills. It would not.

"You wanna take a look?" the man beside him said. He nudged his horse closer to Cole and offered him the glass, encased in bronze. A stark white line divided the suntanned skin on top of his hand, another along the right side of his neck.

"You're going blind, Cutter. I don't need a glass to see that distance."

"Shit, Cole, you didn't have to say that out loud." Cutter glanced suspiciously at Jamie and Bill on Cole's other side. Neither of them paid him any mind. He put the glass back in the inside pocket of his coat, stretching the flap like a wing to reveal the many personal possessions flooding out of the extra pockets he had stitched to it. A drawing of a woman peeked out, only her lined but lovely face visible, black hair touched with gray drawn up in a tight bun.

"They know already, Cutter. Been around you too long not to know. Whole country probably knows by now. Headline in the New York paper, 'Elderly outlaw can't see straight no more'."

"Aw hell." He was silent for a time. "Hey, you think I orta see about gettin' me some glasses? Like reading glasses, but for seeing far. I hear they got them thereabouts."

"Whereabouts?"

"Thereabouts? I don't know."

The train was close enough to see the piled timber across the track at the mouth of the canyon then. It had taken them a day to manage that. The whistle keened. Cole could see it slowing down. He drew his revolver and blasted off twice in the air. Riders suddenly appeared in the tall prairie grass fifty feet out on either side of the train as it stopped. They had coaxed their horses down onto their sides until the train got into position. The train was nearly stopped by the time they caught sight of the riders closing in, too late to pick up speed quickly and there was still the wall of timber blocking their path.

Cole picked his way down the slope, his companions tracing his path behind him. He stopped at a moderate distance and watched his people entering the train cars. Crowboy and Jessie were directing the engineers into the grass at gunpoint while the rest combed the passengers and storage cars, pistols outlined black through the windows against the sunlight. The first-class section would be all folk of wealth and the outlaws would clean them out thoroughly, but they had orders to be observant of who they found in second class seats, to leave be any of apparent lesser means. The emigrant car would go entirely unmolested. His crew was practiced, and they had the whole train swept in less than ten minutes. *That's a new record for them,* he thought. He failed to suppress the small smile that came. The jewels and spare cash they came up with were just extra though. He wouldn't suppress his smile if the take they were promised was as good as they expected it to be.

"Front car's heavy," Bill said. "Gonna be a lot of rings, necklaces, earrings when it comes to count time."

"Pick you out a purty pair," Jaime said.

Guns fired off further down the train and on the other side from them, three shots in the air. He turned his horse south and curled around the tip of the train to ride its length, companions in tow. Figures fanned out around an armored car past the emigrant section. There was a thin glass slit for sight and a metal slide and the big door was securely shut. Young James bounced up to the side, excitable as always, and smacked the butt of his shotgun against the metal twice. "Come on out, piggies! Before we blow the doors off and come in after you!"

Cole reined in a safe distance ahead of the car. He shot a glance left and saw a face duck back below the window. "What's the matter?" Bill asked.

"Feds holed up in here," Young James said. "Thinking I should dynamite it, Cole. What do you think?"

"I say blow that turtle wide open."

A tiny iron slide scraped open. "Hold up! I'm coming out, don't shoot." The big door yawned and a man jerkily stepped down and out.

Young James patted down his pockets and produced a badge. "Pinkerton," he announced, prancing over to hand it up to Cole. Cole fingered the silver insignia and tossed it in the dirt.

"You're Cole Park?" the Pink asked.

"Shoot, I thought we was supposed to be asking the questions here," Young James said. Laughter all around.

Cole looked down at the Pink and crossed his wrists at the saddle horn. "Cole Park I am."

A second man appeared from the shadow of the car, Colt metal flashing in the sunlight. Cole swore and ripped his pistol free as he saw the ignition down the barrel and the burst of gun smoke. *Too slow.* A pistol blasted off to his right and the Pink was thrown back against the train car in the same instant he felt the bullet whistle by his ear. Young James slammed a fist into the other Pink's temple and planted a foot on his back when he hit the ground, double barrel aimed at the base of his skull.

Cole breathed slowly, carefully. *Let that panic go, son. Let it out easy.* It went. "Maybe you're not as blind as I thought, Cutter. You put that one right between his eyes."

Cutter shrugged and holstered his gun. "Nah, you had me pegged alright, Cole. I can see pretty good at this distance though."

"Still quicker than a rattlesnake."

"Yeah, that's about right."

"What about this one?" Young James said. "Want me to blast him one? Don't you dare think I won't do it either, pig. I'll do it with the biggest grin you never seen." Cole could hear the hot rage bubbling up with every word. *He's pissed he let that one happen. Good. An almost situation isn't as good a lesson as a done deal, but there's some gain there anyway.*

Cole ignored Young James and addressed their prisoner. "What's your name, Pink?"

"Preston Whitman." Behind Whitman, Sullam and Chester had cleared the car for any more lurking Pinkertons and had the dead one by a leg each, dragging him off the car floor. He hit the dirt with a gout of dust. His blood trail glinted and dripped off the edge of the car to drizzle the dead man's face. Daiyu climbed in to quest after what they were escorting.

Cole looked at the living Pinkerton for a while. "If I ask you some questions, Mr. Whitman, are you gonna answer?"

"Nope," Preston snarled.

Cole sighed. *Today feels like a day made for sighs.* "Didn't think so. Scalp his friend, put 'em both on a horse and send 'em back east."

Preston started to rise, but Young James clamped a hand around the back of his neck and held him there. Preston snarled, "Shoulda figured you for a savage bastard when you got Indians and Chinamen and Negros and even goddamn women doing your murdering for you. Now you're scalping lawmen."

Cole grinned, then let a chuckle burst free.

"What's funny?"

"Oh, it's just awful amusing how often I hear agents of the most savage force on the continent accusing me of savagery. Hell, we even did that man the courtesy of killing him before we take his hair. Seems downright high-mannered to me."

"Ain't even lawmen anyway," Bill said. "Pinkerton is a private agency."

"They're private when anyone suggests some federal oversight might be worth a think, but lawmen whenever it suits them to invoke a higher authority."

"Pigs every day of the week whichever way they wanna put it," Cutter said.

Jamie shimmied down off her horse and stalked over to the dead Pinkerton while Young James walked his companion over to one of their spare horses. Jamie took him by the legs and pulled him away from the car a few feet, then circled around behind him. She twisted her fingers in the dead man's scruffy black hair and pulled him up to a sitting position, his legs jutting out at ninety-degree angles, arms twisted up awkwardly at his side. Her knife came whistling from its sheath. "Hey Bill, gonna set a record with this pig, keep them peepers on me," she said, flashing a lopsided grin.

Bill spat. "I'll believe it when I see it."

Cole cut in. "No records this time, Jaime. Just get me a nice clean scalp. We're sending a message, not trying to make an early supper."

"You got it." He saw her lips pout just a little before she set to work. She slit a seam along the dead man's hairline with a single sure movement. Her fingers tangled up in the corpse's hair and pulled hard, not jerking and not as hard as she would have in another situation to see the trophy won faster. She used the knife to peel it up until she reached the half-hidden bald spot and then cut another line left to right there and ripped the scalp free. The corpse's head slumped over above his lap, his body awkwardly holding itself up in a sitting position like a pouting child that had just fallen asleep in place. He looked at the red, dripping skull cap and felt a little tickle of nausea. He suspected he would never get used to the sight of the skinny young woman taking hair.

Jaime inspected her work. "Well, I didn't set a record on time, but I figure I did on quality. That there's a beaut." She handed the trophy gingerly to Chester, who walked it over to the unfortunate Mr. Whitman, dangling it carefully away from his body by a few hairs.

Daiyu had reappeared from the shaded train car with a small iron safe box under her arm. "What you got there, Daiyu?" Bill called to her.

"Cash and railroad bonds. Lot of money in this little thing," she said, flashing Bill a wink. His eyes followed her all the way to her horse, where she tied it on with her saddlebags.

They mounted Preston on the horse with wrists tied together around the reins and his legs across his horse's belly so he could neither dismount nor remove the scalp hanging from his neck. They had stripped off his coat but left him with the rest of his clothes and his sharp bowler hat. "Give him a sip of water before you send him off," Cole said. They pressed a skin to his lips for a few moments and set his mount trotting down the train track back east. *Some savage I am,* he thought.

"Wish I could see the boss bastard's face when that nag comes trotting into town," Bill said.

"Me too. They'll be coming for us before long though."

"I'll get a look when they do then. Hey, hand that up here, Crowboy."

Cole looked down at the passing youth holding up a big cloth sack. "Bring it here first, if you would. I'd like to have an idea how much Bill's skimmed later." He sifted through the pile of assorted jewelry, cash and coin jumbled at the bottom of the sack and handed it to Bill, satisfied. He looked down the track and watched the distance between him and Mr. Whitman grow larger and larger. "Get everyone ready to go," he said to Bill, who set to hollering at the crew until everyone was firmly planted back on a horse. They trotted back up the line.

Cole scanned the windows of the train. The faces staring back at him were largely fearful. One woman near the front of the first-class car gave him pause. She had to be well into her forties, close to two decades his senior at least, but she looked at him with dignified disdain from beneath a wide-brimmed white hat. *Thank ya, ma'am. Your jewels will buy us supper back in Black Birch.* He grinned at her and her lips curled further down in frank distaste and she looked away.

His gaze drifted towards the next car and held in the gap between, stabbing at the prairie gold beyond. A woman stood among grass that came up to her chest. She was far, but he saw her well somehow, saw her black hair hanging loose and ragged around her face and the iron round on her forehead with red streaming down to her lips. She had his eyes.

He looked away.

"Let's get gone."

They rode in column back up the hills where Cole had taken his vantage with a hundred pairs of eyes on their backs. From there they would venture down a half-hidden little track through the mountains heading west, an uncomfortable ride that they would have to endure in single file, but one from which they wouldn't be tracked. They left their mess across the mouth of the lower pass, in no rush to see the train moving again. If they had the luxury, Cole would have watched those wealthy passengers disembark, strip out of their expensive coats, and sweat away the work of clearing the track and he would have done it smiling, but he knew they needed to make some distance while they could. Town was a couple of days' ride in the other direction and poor Preston Whitman would be seeing his direct superior before dusk, like as not. And when he did, they would come after them in force, pistols and buck knives on every belt, rifles sheathed on every saddle.

Cole let his crew start down the track and paused on the hill to look out over the prairie one last time. The smog of industry was visible, miles distant, over the low mountains on the other side. He imagined the prairie grass trampled flat with a black wave of mounted Pinkertons, slavering at his scent like hounds. In his mind's eye, they went out of their way to ride over every inch of that landscape and leave it blasted and desolate, conquering the land a second time as their forefathers had done. It was a bad thought, but he smiled. *Hope to see you soon.*

CHAPTER TWO

They rode well past dusk into the roiling, reaching dark by the seeking light of torches, far off the well-worn roads and onto the wild tracks of beasts to make enough distance for comfort. At the moment of true dusk, they had turned their path hard north towards some hillier ground and made their camp when their near blindness brought them to the end of the flat landscape. It was not fear of the Pinkertons' competence that drove them to such measures, but a healthy respect for caution and the unpredictability of fate, two things all outlaws should mind. They all slept much better for it.

Cole sat by his fire, warming himself from the sudden night chill that had set in. His gun lay in pieces across a bit of cloth in the dirt, freshly cleaned and oiled, the six bullets laid out in a neat row. Cutter had lain down across from him, head propped against his bedroll, reading a dime novel about outlaws. It seemed a formidable irony, and a better joke, but Cole knew he truly enjoyed the stories. He listened to the sounds of the fire talk, the jokes and stories, and looked out into the darkness. Only the smallest kiss of moonlight slipped through the cloud cover, but it was enough to set the darkness rippling like the deep ocean, concealing all manner of things.

He rose and walked softly and quietly in the shaded areas between the campfires and watched them. He listened to Mikey on his fiddle, making Theresa and Annie dance in the flickering light, their shadows a more maniacal mirror to them in the beyond. Crowboy helped Jeffrey with his sums, tallying their take. Bill hovered nearby, ostensibly to offer input, but his eyes cut in every free instant to Daiyu where she played checkers with Geming. Sullam, Chester, and Sarah watched silently beside them, hovering like children. Jaime scraped a whetstone against her knife again and again, firelight glinting in her eyes, reflecting back darkly. Young James lay back at the edge of the light in his bedroll, smoldering.

He was reminded not for the first time of how different they were, the places they sprang from. They had warriors and killers, helpers and healers. Some were colder than others, some were kinder. Each road walked to find this one shared soul had been singular. And yet they had pulled together inexorably across this continent. More than two dozen unique beginnings to one common destination. For what they did share was that there was no other place for them.

———

HE WOKE up some hours later when the bushes rustled near his bedroll, and he came up with pistol cocked and pointed into the darkness. He listened, ears reaching for every sound, but nothing more came. He stood up and scanned what he could with the slim moonlight and saw a strange light on some distant hillside, gleaming, calling like a star. As he watched, it seemed to rise higher and higher before finally blinking out.

He wiped a chill night sweat from his face and thought, *Get yourself together, Cole. Hell of a time to be losing your mind, you've got people counting on you.* He looked to one of the other fires, smoldering low, and saw a slender woman in a pale blue dress standing on the other side of the coals, watching him. Blood drizzled down her face to the tip of her sharp chin and his gun hand started shaking. Low to himself, he said, "Not. Now." He lay back down in his bedroll and set his gun beside him. The stars were out, but he forced his eyes closed.

END

ACKNOWLEDGMENTS

My thanks to everyone who ever handed, bought, or pointed me to a story.

ABOUT THE AUTHOR

Brett Tharp is a writer of historical horror and dark fantasy. His short fiction has been published by Frontier Tales and Night Terror Novels. He lives in southeast Missouri.

www.ingramcontent.com/pod-product-compliance
Lightning Source LLC
Chambersburg PA
CBHW071530100726
47908CB00004B/1346